FEUD ALONG THE DEARBORN

Until the night of the fire, Stanton, Montana, was a peaceful town. Its marshal, Silas Tasker, rejoiced in the knowledge that he had rid the town of the kind of rip-roaring reputation attributed to so many other cattle-towns across the west. But in the aftermath of the blaze that destroyed the barn on the Diamond-H ranch, a man lost his sanity, others died, and Silas found himself confronted with a feud capable of developing into an unstoppable range-war.

WILL DuREY

FEUD
ALONG THE
DEARBORN

Complete and Unabridged

LINFORD
Leicester

First published in Great Britain in 2018 by
Robert Hale
an imprint of The Crowood Press
Wiltshire

First Linford Edition
published 2021
by arrangement with The Crowood Press
Wiltshire

A catalogue record for this book is available
from the British Library.

ISBN 978–1–4448–4677–5

Published by
Ulverscroft Limited
Anstey, Leicestershire

Printed and bound in Great Britain by
TJ Books Ltd., Padstow, Cornwall

This book is printed on acid-free paper

1

Mary Hoag chased the released horses across the yard, urging them towards the open gate that led onto the meadowland beyond. Her shouts and arm waving, however, were virtually unnecessary; already the animals were running for their lives, panic-stricken by the flames that were leaping into the blackness above the timber building in which they'd recently been stabled. Their sounds of fright and flight, snorts, neighs and the rapid drumming hoof beats, mingled with the crackling of burning wood and the yells of Mary's father and elder brother who were fighting the fire at her back. Matty Slade, the cook, and the other hands who had been roused from their sleep by the general hubbub and the terror-bearing shouts of 'Fire!' were racing from the distant bunkhouse to aid in the battle required to prevent the inferno spreading to other buildings.

Occasional gusts of wind acted like bellows, fanning the flames, enabling them to climb and consume the walls until they flicked high above the building, slashing the black sky like the blades of angry swordsmen. Smoke curled and spread as it, too, succumbed to the vagaries of the breeze, and mixed within it was the hot ash and small fragments of burning wood capable of extending the fire to the nearby barns or even the Hoags' home.

With the horses careering off into the night and safe from danger, Mary hurried back across the yard to assist in the fight against the fire. She tightened the shawl that she'd flung around her shoulders before leaving the house so that it didn't become an encumbrance when she began raising water from the well. It had been the only additional item of clothing she'd had time to collect after being roused from her bed by the barking of the house dog and the high whinnying of the trapped horses, but she had little need of it for warmth.

Although she was separated from the burning building by thirty yards, she felt enshrouded by the heat it emitted. Her thoughts flew to the predicament of her father and brother, knowing that despite the intense heat and choking smoke that swirled around them, they would continue to struggle against losing the stable until all hope of saving it had gone. She could see them, little more than silhouettes against the orange light of the blazing building, striving to find a place to launch a counter-attack, some weakness in the fire that would give them a chance of defeating it and protecting the rest of their property. She hurried on, determined to do her part. She was capable of hauling the water from the ground for the men to fling against the burning timbers.

Already it had been a day of troubles for the Hoag family, but they had been minor irritations in comparison to this conflagration. Earlier, in Stanton, Mary had been at the centre of a confronta-

3

tion between her father and Walt Risby. Many people regarded Walt as a selfish, arrogant bully, a reputation which had recently been endorsed by leaving his friend, Jimmy Carson, afoot a day shy of town. To Walt it had been nothing more than a prank but with recent rumours of Arapaho raids in the area, few people had agreed with him. Mary liked Walt. He wasn't perfect, but neither was she and, limited by the small number of young men in the vicinity, she found his antics more amusing than aggressively unkind. Since the death of her ma there was little more to her life than work from sunup to sundown; a chance meeting with Walt always brightened her day. He was flirtatious, but she didn't suppose for one moment that she was being favoured above any other girl in the territory.

Ben Hoag, however, didn't share his daughter's opinion and had given voice to his objections when he'd found them in conversation outside the general store. Several bystanders had overheard his tirade, which had not only been a rant against the young man's character, but also a warning to stay away from his daughter.

Although Walt's wild reputation had been used as the stick with which to beat him, Mary knew that that was not the root cause of her father's objection. Over the years, he and Mort Risby had had many disagreements over land and cattle, and though neither man had current cause to be at war with the other, their peace had not brought about anything more than a tenuous friendship. At home, Mary had harangued her father on the subject, laying out her own point of view, but he had been obdurate in his opinion that until Walt Risby showed some evidence of sense and humanity, he would not be welcome in their home. Rather than pacifying her father as she'd intended, Mary's defence of the young man had made him grouchier, but it was her younger brother, Frank, who bore the brunt of their parent's agitation.

For the best part of a week, Frank's mood had been sullen, his attention to tasks around the ranch suffering from his lax attitude. It was an attitude that rankled his father and angry words had been exchanged more than once during the preceding days, but that night Ben Hoag had predicted that if his son didn't change his ways, he would end up a ne'er-do-well like Walt Risby and had ordered him to take the night-watch, nursing the herd on the home slopes that overlooked the ranch.

Now, as she raised a bucketful of water from the well, Mary wondered why her younger brother hadn't returned to the ranch - the fire would be visible for many miles. It was even possible that the whinnying of the frightened horses could have reached him on the hillside, before disturbing the sleepers in the house. She cast a glance over her shoulder. Only an ominous darkness lay beyond the yard rails. Despite the fire's heat, it seemed to Mary that her body shivered with a sudden chill, a portent of more trouble.

The trouble, however, wasn't at Mary's back, it was being carried on the latest gust of wind blowing along the valley. A glowing ember, collected from the crumbling stable, was floating across the ranchyard like a giant firefly and became entangled in the folds of her cotton nightdress. Instantly, the material began to burn. Alarmed, she started to beat the flames with her hands, but they didn't diminish. Instead, they grew with frightening speed. By the time her first scream reached the men-folk, she was a flaming torch. Her clothing and hair were aflame, and the torment of her pain echoed in the cries that were receding from screams to horrible, gargled moans.

A moment of stunned disbelief transfixed Ben Hoag and his eldest son, Tom. Then they ran, the battle to save the stable overtaken by their need to protect something more precious. Tom held a thick horse-blanket that he'd rescued from the stable, and while he was yet ten strides from his sister, prepared to throw it over her. The men who were racing from the bunkhouse, changed course, too.

Young Chet Taylor reached Mary first. He began scooping dirt over her in an effort to extinguish the flames that still leapt around her body.

Mary writhed on the ground, her right arm raised towards Chet in supplication. Like the rest of her body, it was charred and blistered, twisted as though melted into disfigurement. Her eyes were wide, protruding in an ugly, haunted manner, and her mouth too, was agape as though needing to give voice to a thousand screams, but only low moans of hellish torment were able to escape.

Chet ceased his labour when Tom smothered Mary under the blanket. Tom hoped this action would kill the flames and save his sister from further injury, but he really wasn't sure if he was helping or heaping more distress upon her. In truth, he had no knowledge of the best course of action to follow. Over the years, there had been minor burns aplenty, treatable with salves of aloe vera or chamomile, sometimes with mutton tallow and beeswax or even the white of an egg, but Mary's injuries were of an altogether different nature. He had never seen anyone consumed by fire and although covering his sister with the blanket successfully extinguished the flames, he was sure he was inflicting further damage. He had the notion that he was tearing the skin from her body. 'Get the doctor,' he yelled to no one in particular.

It was Chet who accepted the command, running off to the corral behind the bunkhouse where the working ponies were kept. It wasn't that he was the best rider, simply that he welcomed the opportunity to put distance between himself and Mary. He'd carried a secret torch for his boss's daughter since arriving at the ranch, and the sight of her suffering and his inability to end it, filled him with horror. He hadn't the skills to provide Mary with any measure of comfort, but he was willing and able to fetch the one person who perhaps could. Nothing could be done now to save the stable and it seemed that the fear of it spreading to the other buildings had been dismissed because, as he saddled up, he could hear Ben Hoag insisting that his daughter was taken to the house. Chet couldn't imagine how that could be achieved without inflicting even more pain on the injured girl, all he knew was that it was essential to get Doc Brewster back to the ranch quickly.

Stanton was a four-mile ride. Chet spurred the cayuse under him as soon as he was on its back. The horse was at full gallop before they passed through the open gate. As he turned the horse towards town he was aware of another rider coming down from the northern slopes at a reckless speed. He guessed it was Frank Hoag, summoned away from his nightwatch of the cattle by the leaping flames but he didn't slacken his pace to inform him of his sister's injury. He yelled in the horse's ear and rode pell-mell in search of the doctor.

2

Mary Hoag died before the sun had climbed above the eastern horizon to spread its light on the jumble of buildings that constituted the Diamond-H ranch. Abraham Brewster, the long-serving doctor to the township of Stanton, had reached the place less than an hour earlier, his old, two-wheeled buggy slewing to an awkward halt at the end of a frantic journey. The doctor had driven in Chet Taylor's wake, his vehicle bouncing, swinging and swerving over every inch of the four-mile journey as his old mare tried to keep pace with the cowboy's onrushing pony. The smell of burning wood had filled his nostrils for almost half the distance and when he'd clattered up to the ranch-house door, he'd leapt from the buggy with as much agility as his old bones permitted, leaving Chet to tend to the lathered animals.

Matty Slade was on the porch with

Buck Downs, another ranch-hand, but they had no words of greeting to offer the doctor as he hurried past and into the house. There was little need for words however, their sunken-eyed expressions were sufficient to convey the hopelessness of the situation before the medical man even opened the door. Mary lay on the table, a pillow under her head. She was unconscious; pain and shock had taken away her senses. For her father this was both a blessing and a worry; the deep, preternatural sounds that had issued forth from his daughter's mouth when they'd carried her inside were now at an end, but the ensuing silence only generated a different cause for alarm, one which he could barely contemplate. Ben's wide-eyed stare emphasised for Abe Brewster the fear that gripped the rancher; that never having asked for help in the past, he had no idea how to ask or beg for it now that he needed it so badly. Abe Brewster noted the unexpected trails on the rancher's cheeks, two thin lines that had washed a way through the smoke and ash particles covering his face. Ben Hoag had no remembrance of shedding tears, but they'd fallen steadily while he'd tended to his daughter. He was a tough man, had been hard in the rearing of his sons, but his daughter had forever been the recipient of his tenderness. His inability to cure her or even offer comfort, put him in desperate straits. It was Matty Slade who'd advised covering her with a soothing ointment and, unable to find anything better, had brought lard from his cookhouse supplies. Ben had applied it thickly, agonizing over every handful, unsure of the efficacy of the treatment, fearing he was inflicting greater harm to the horrifically-damaged, slight body. Now, Mary lay still and ghastly white and all her father's hopes for her recovery were vested in Abe Brewster's knowledge.

It wasn't enough. Neither Abe's experience nor anything his bag contained, were capable of assisting Mary's fight against her injuries. Her heart succumbed to the excessive demands placed on it by her failing organs. She died without ever regaining consciousness, her final convulsion witnessed by Doc Brewster, her father and her brothers.

Frank had reached the ranch, riding as though all the demons of Hell were at his back. In the house, the sight of his sister's ruined body provided unwanted confirmation of the news Matty Slade had imparted beyond the door. He found it difficult to drag his gaze away from the blistered face twisted by the agonies she'd suffered. Transfixed, his inability to find any words capable of expressing his inner desolation only added to the heavy silence within the room.

It was Abe Brewster who spoke first. Gathering his hat and bag, he prepared to leave. 'I'm sorry, Ben, but no matter how quickly I'd got here, I wouldn't have been able to save her. The damage was too severe.'

Ben Hoag raised his eyes from the spot on the floor he'd been staring at for several minutes, but his gaze didn't settle on the doctor's face. Instead, he was

14

looking over his shoulder at his youngest son who remained rooted to the spot a couple of steps inside the room. 'Where were you?' he asked, his voice quiet but deep, like the rumble of distant, approaching thunder. 'Why didn't you raise a warning? Up on the hillside you must have seen the flames before anyone else. Why didn't you come to help? Were you asleep?'

'Pa!' It was Tom who interjected, annoyed by the gruffness in his father's voice. He knew that Mary had always been the old man's favourite, but he wasn't the only one affected by her loss. This was not the time to renew the petty argument that had led to Frank's earlier abasement, riding nightguard. Whatever reason he had for his absence from fighting the fire, its explanation could wait for another day.

Ben Hoag wiped aside his eldest son's intervention with a wave of his arm. He rose to his feet and took a couple of steps towards Frank, his head thrust forward in characteristically aggressive style. 'Your sister's dead because she was doing your job,' he snapped at the youngest Hoag, anger blazing in his eyes. 'Where were you?'

Colour rose in Frank Hoag's face. In his whole life, he couldn't recall one word of praise from his father. From childhood, he'd worked hard and become as capable a ranch-hand as any of those employed in recent years. He earned his keep; working cattle, repairing fences and breaking-in horses from day-break to sun-down, but only his mistakes attracted his father's attention. The rest of the time he was just doing what was expected of him, attending to the multitude of chores that were necessary to maintain the profitability of the small ranch.

Again, Tom was first to respond. He was the senior son by eight years. He couldn't remember a day when he hadn't worked alongside his father, not only learning the essential physical skills but also adhering to his parent's philosophy that if their inheritance was to have any value after he'd gone, then the development of the ranch ought to be the primary concern of his sons. Until his younger brother's recent bouts of moodiness, Ben's unencouraging manner had barely mattered to Tom. Indeed, he had always been too busy to recognize the trait and although Frank's increasingly voluble grumbling had forced him to recognize his father's unyielding attitude, it hadn't persuaded him that there was any fault in his behaviour. Lately, however, it had become necessary for Tom to act as buffer between his father and younger brother. 'It was an accident, Pa. Mary's decision to fight the fire had nothing to do with Frank's absence. She was as eager as you and I to protect the stock.'

'Yes, you and I, but not him.' He pointed a stubby finger at his youngest son. 'He was asleep somewhere on the hillside or perhaps watching from a safe distance.'

This accusation riled Frank but not because of its inaccuracy. He hadn't been asleep or watching the flames leaping into the sky, but the truth wouldn't elevate him in his father's esteem. He couldn't tell him that he'd deserted the herd to spend the dark hours at the home of a woman whose husband was out of town. Ben Hoag would regard both of those actions as a betrayal of the principles he'd sought to instil in his son. If he ever learned the reason for Frank's absence, he would never forgive him.

'I saw someone hanging around the herd,' he said, hoping the lie would deflate his father's anger.

'Rustlers?' asked Tom.

'That's what I suspected,' Frank answered, but thinking fast, added, 'but I only saw one rider which was why I followed him.'

'Did you recognize him?' asked Tom. Frank shook his head.

'Did you catch him?'

'No. He headed south, through the bluffs. I trailed him almost to the Dearborn.'

'Difficult following a man at night through that territory.'

Frank agreed, but having begun the lie, found himself embellishing it to justify an absence from the ranch sufficient to cover the fire that had destroyed the stables and taken his sister's life. 'I lost him a couple of times, but I caught a glimpse of his horse's white tail which kept me on his trail.'

'White tail!' The words were spoken by Ben Hoag. The brothers turned their attention to their father whose face bore a look of savagery.

Instantly, Frank knew that he was no longer the object of his father's anger, yet he was gripped with the certainty that the lie which had been uttered to avoid trouble had, in fact, intensified the possibility.

'Only one white horse around here,' snarled Ben. 'That colt belonging to Walt Risby,' he added unnecessarily.

Hurriedly, Frank tried to divert his father's train of thought. 'It might not have been a white horse,' he said. 'All I saw was its rear, its tail.'

Dismissive of his son's interruption,

Ben Hoag spoke again, expanding on his belief that the nightrider had been Walt Risby. 'He wasn't here to rustle our cattle, he came to wreak revenge for being humiliated when we met in Stanton. He put a flame to our stable.'

Brushing aside the initial protestations of his sons, he expounded on the charge with an attack on Walt Risby's character.

Both Tom and Frank opposed their father's accusation. 'I didn't get close enough to identify the rider,' said Frank. 'Besides, he was heading south towards the Dearborn. That's the wrong direction for either Stanton or his home.'

'Who else has a grudge against this family?' demanded Ben. 'And all the district has been waiting for him to commit a criminal act. He's been close to it several times.'

Tom interceded, attempting to curb his father's unjustified allegations. 'Walt's a little wild, Pa, but he hasn't done anything to cause Marshal Tasker to lock him up.'

Doc Brewster had finished tending to

Mary's body. He'd draped it in a blanket and now awaited the assistance of someone in the family to move it onto the bed in her room. At present, however, its silent presence dominated the room and Ben looked down on the horrifically scarred face of the daughter he'd loved. He wasn't in a mood to be pacified by his eldest son or anyone else. 'He's done something now,' he said. 'He's killed your sister and I'll see him hang for it.'

Dawn's strengthening light illuminated Stanton's long Main Street as Doc Brewster reached town. His return had been undertaken at a less perilous pace than that which had taken him out to the Hoag ranch, but even so, his arms ached from the pull on the reins and his eyes were heavy with sleep. When he'd first settled in this part of Montana he'd easily shrugged off the effects of an all-night vigil while attending to the needs of a patient. Then, he'd accepted it as an essential part of his calling; now, as the years advanced, it induced a disconcerting weariness, invoking an acknowledgement that even this man of medicine was mortal and subject to the limitations wrought by a lifetime full of care and concern for those in need of his expertise. Like his old horse, he was keen to reach familiar surroundings. He knew that when she heard him unharnessing Singer in the small stable behind their house, his wife would begin to brew up a fresh pot of coffee to welcome him home. It was her usual practice and, in normal circumstances, one which he welcomed. This morning, however, he knew it would have scant effect in filling the emptiness that had gripped him during the previous hours. Despite the many years he'd spent treating sickness, injuries and fatalities, he was still saddened by Mary Hoag's dreadful death. He'd watched the pleasant and popular young woman grow from childhood, and knew her undeserving of the torment she'd undoubtedly endured during her final minutes of life. Yet it wasn't the horrific manner of her death that troubled him most; her father's words of vengeance had echoed in his mind again and again during the drive back to Stanton. Everyone in the vicinity was aware that Ben Hoag had doted on his daughter, and in Doc Brewster's opinion it was natural for him to be staggered by her loss, but his grief had affected his reason and with unswerving certitude, had attached the blame for Mary's death onto Walt Risby. Before he could put his feet up and partake of Alice's kitchen fare, Abe Brewster felt it his duty to report the matter to the marshal.

At this early hour, Abe wasn't sure where he would find Silas Tasker. Sometimes the lawman slept in the Stanton Hotel bedroom provided by the town as part of his salary, and some nights he bedded down on one of the bunks in the cells behind his office. He hoped it didn't become necessary to look further afield because that would involve a visit to Lily Cregar's place and she objected vocally and often violently to any disruption to the morning peace she enjoyed with her girls after a busy night in the various saloons around town. To the doctor's surprise, he found the marshal leaning against a post outside his office.

For weeks now, a growing restlessness had dragged the marshal early from his bed. In the first light of day he had taken to surveying the quiet main street, remembering its frontier raucousness when he'd arrived, and pondering his future now that the town was a haven of civilization. Five years earlier he'd been one of the county deputies supporting Sheriff Brown who'd been summoned to quell a possible range war. Accusations of water poisoning, stream diversions, and stock stampedes in order to grab land from his neighbours had been levelled at Mort Risby. When their opposition developed into a series of violent confrontations, the diplomatic Sheriff Brown arrived to investigate and adjudicate. The matter was resolved without arrests or punishments but, at the conclusion of the affair, the people of Stanton were reluctant to see their town totally abandoned by professional lawmen. Silas had accepted the post of town marshal and been the guardian of its laws ever since.

Although his authority didn't officially spread beyond the town's limits, his presence in Stanton had a calming effect on the surrounding territory. This was due in no small part to the fact that Stanton's reputation as a wild and open town was gradually repressed, allowing the more refined pursuits proposed by the town council, to flourish. Silas Tasker's role in the civic advancement of Stanton was acknowledged.

The town's advancement, however, was not matched by his own prosperity. He was in his fortieth year and the prospect of achieving anything more than the pittance of a marshal's salary became more remote every day. Even finding a wife had escaped him, those women who weren't already married were rarely of a suitable age. There was nothing to keep him in this town. It was time to move on before he lost that urge in life to discover the grass on the far side of the hill.

'You're up and about early, Doc,' he

said as the buggy was halted outside his office.

'Got called out during the night,' replied the medical man. 'A fire at the Hoag place.'

'Somebody hurt?'

Abe related the details of Mary Hoag's death to the lawman. It was the marshal's duty to maintain the official record of such events in the district, but he heard the doctor's story with grimmer attention than he might have done for a different victim. Silas was almost twice Mary Hoag's age, but his eyes had long alighted on her with favour. It was his own nomadic history that had prevented him from making any attempt to form a special attachment with Mary. Although he'd lived in Stanton for four years, he wasn't yet certain that he wouldn't awaken one morning, saddle-up and leave this town far behind. He hadn't been in one place so long since enlisting in the army in '63. It was through a haze of disbelief that he heard Abe Brewster impart his concern about Ben Hoag's intentions.

'Young Frank didn't identify Walt Risby,' said the doctor, 'but Ben's got it fixed in his mind that there isn't another white-tailed horse around here. It's fixed in his mind that Walt started the fire as some kind of retribution for their earlier confrontation.'

Silas was ignorant of the event to which Abe Brewster referred and it was necessary for the doctor to elucidate. The marshal found it difficult to believe that Walt Risby would react in such a manner.

'Walt's a bit of a wild one but not in a malicious way.'

'That's what Tom told his father, but Ben is adamant. He won't listen to any plea of mitigation. He believes Walt Risby set fire to his property and as a result, his daughter is dead. He wants revenge, Silas, and I think he'd prefer to dish out his own punishment.'

'Thanks for the warning, Doc. I'll try to defuse the situation. I'll ride out to the Risby place and give

Walt the opportunity to supply an alibi.'

3

A crew of four were working cattle on the open range west of Stanton. Two of the cowboys were cutting out steers and hauling them towards a small fire where the others were waiting to hog-tie them then burn the mark of the Triple-R into the hide above their right hind-leg. Sitting a little apart from them, their boss, Mort Risby, watched contentedly, aware that his stock was in capable hands. Using a large, red handkerchief, he wiped the inside of his hat, drying off the moisture that had accumulated during the morning. It was while he was replacing his headgear that he became aware of the approaching rider. He lifted a hand to shield his eyes against the sun's glare in an effort to identify the newcomer.

Silas Tasker had slowed his horse to walking pace when he came alongside the cattle and was progressing towards Mort Risby as gently as a herder on a stormy night who feared the risk of stampeding the herd. But the animals weren't the marshal's concern. He'd already recognized the burly figure of the Triple-R ranch owner but needed to scrutinize the other faces. Failing to find the man he was seeking, he drew to a halt alongside Mort.

Mort Risby greeted him affably. 'Morning, Silas. Not often we see you outside town limits.'

Silas Tasker removed his hat and wiped his sleeved forearm across his brow. 'I'm looking for your boy,' he said. 'Need to talk with him.'

The rancher appraised the lawman with a steely gaze. 'Something wrong?' he asked.

'I'm not sure. That's why I'm here, to hear Walt's story.'

'Concerning what?'

'Boy's old enough to talk for himself,' Silas said. 'Reckon I'll keep my questions for him.'

Mort stiffened his spine, raising him an inch or two in the saddle. 'If you're fixing to accuse him of something, you'd better tell me about it.'

'Didn't say I was. I just want to know if he was hanging around the Hoag place last night.'

'What reason would he have for doing that?'

'That's what I mean to ask.'

'Well, he wasn't.'

'You seem pretty sure about that, Mort.'

'I am. He's in Miles City conducting business on my behalf with the Cattlemen's Association.'

Silas received the news with a great deal of relief. During the ride from town, the suggestion that Walt Risby had deliberately started a fire on Ben Hoag's property, had tumbled over and over in his mind. Overall, he'd doubted that the young man was responsible; Walt was full of youthful devilment but that fell far short of the callous nature required to put at risk another man's property and stock. Besides, Ben Hoag wasn't the first father to put a flea in Walt's ear about his relationship with their daughters and he'd merely laughed off those incidents without either offending the father or diminishing his attentions to the daughter. Fun filled his life and he spread it around Stanton at every opportunity.

Still, it wasn't Silas's personal opinion that had brought him this far from town, he was the marshal and it was his duty to investigate crimes and uphold the law. It was fixed in Ben Hoag's mind that Walt Risby was guilty of the deed and, according to Doctor Brewster, was seeking revenge for Mary's death. Silas was prepared to attribute Ben's rants to grief, but he couldn't let them develop into action. Presenting the bereaved rancher with evidence of Walt's innocence would put an end to the threats.

'When did he go?' asked Silas.

Unexpectedly, Mort Risby bristled at the question. 'You doubting my word?'

'No. I'm asking questions to establish facts. I need information to appease Ben Hoag.'

'What's it got to do with Ben? Why

should my boy's whereabouts be of interest to him?'

Silas pushed his hat back and dragged his forearm once more across his brow. The action wasn't primarily to dry the sweat from his brow, more to give him a moment to think, to decide how much of the situation he should impart to the other man.

'Speak up,' Mort insisted. 'Whatever has happened had nothing to do with Walt. These men,' he indicated the two at the fire who had been paying interest to the conversation since the marshal's arrival, 'will confirm that Walt left the ranch shortly after noon yesterday.'

Silas acknowledged the nods of agreement that Luke Bywater and Chuck Grainger aimed in his direction. 'A stable caught fire over at the Hoag place last night,' he said. 'Young Frank spotted a rider on a white horse close to their ranch.'

'And you thought it was Walt!'

'I didn't say that, but I do need to know where he was when the fire began.'

'Are you saying it was a deliberate act?'

'That hasn't been established.'

'But that is what Ben thinks.'

'Seems that him and Walt argued yesterday morning in Stanton.'

It was clear from the stoic expression on Mort's face that he was unaware of an angry exchange between the two men. He turned his eyes on Luke Bywater.

'Didn't amount to anything, Mr Risby. Walt was talking to Mary, teasing her, as he does. Mr Hoag thought he'd overstepped the mark. Warned him to stay away from his daughter in future. Don't think either Walt or Mary Hoag took it seriously.'

Mort muttered. 'Girls! They'll be the death of him.' More loudly, he addressed his next words at the marshal. 'He didn't show any sign of annoyance before leaving for Miles City. I doubt if he gave it a moment of consideration.'

'I'll speak to Ben Hoag, tell him that Walt's out of the area. That should appease him, but it'll probably be best to tell Walt to keep clear of him for a few days when he returns home.'

'My boy'll do or go where he pleases. Ben Hoag has no business accusing him of anything. Walt wouldn't start a fire on another man's land and certainly wouldn't endanger the animals. If he continues spreading those false stories, then you can tell Ben Hoag that I'll be the one he'll be having an argument with.' He paused a moment then spoke again, his anger unhidden. 'I guess I'll ride over there now and tell him myself.'

'No!' the marshal's sudden shouted exclamation not only surprised Mort Risby, but caused Luke and Chuck to straighten from their work as though their intervention might be necessary to protect their boss. 'No,' Silas repeated in a more conciliatory tone. 'Don't go over there today. Abe Brewster said they don't want any visitors today.'

'The doctor! Was someone hurt fighting the fire?'

Silas nodded. 'A spark settled on Mary's clothing. By the time Abe got to the ranch it was too late to help her.

They're burying her next to her mother later today.'

The lines of anger that had begun to deepen on Mort's face, now fled as first disbelief, then sympathy chased them away. His opinion of Mary Hoag was no different to that of most people around Stanton; he'd always considered her to be one of the most likeable people in the neighbourhood. In contemplative silence, he watched as Silas turned his horse and headed back to town.

Earlier that morning, Buck Downs and Chet Taylor had offered to dig Mary's grave, but it was a task that the Hoag brothers wouldn't relinquish. Tom and Frank had dug their first grave seven years earlier, laying their mother to rest in the grove that stood three hundred yards north of the ranch-house. They were adamant that their sister was deserving of equal consideration. Over the years, the land had settled, leaving no tell-tale mound to indicate the exact location of the earlier site but the timber board that bore her name and the extent of her days, still stood firm in the ground thereby providing adequate guidance for their excavation. Mary would lie side-by-side with her mother.

In silence, the three men of the Hoag family carried Mary's canvas-wrapped body to the grove and put her carefully into the prepared hole, their gentleness reflecting the care and tenderness she'd bestowed on them since the death of her mother. Before they began to shovel the soil back into the grave, Tom and Frank paused in anticipation of some words from their father, but he could recall only a few sentences he'd heard spoken at other burials he'd attended and swiftly motioned for them to complete the job. He spoke when they set aside the shovels, uttering an oath he deemed binding on his sons but which he wanted no one else to hear. 'I swear, Mary, that your death will not go unpunished. Walt Risby will pay for this deed even if I have to hang him from a tree myself.' The tenor of his voice invited neither comment nor contradiction, and the abrupt manner of his departure from the grove emphasised his patriarchal authority.

Even so, Frank took a hurried step in pursuit, his mouth working to find words of protest, words that would deflect his father from the pursuance of the oath he'd sworn. Tom caught his arm and held on to it when his younger brother tried to shake himself free.

'Not now,' he said. 'Let him go. Let him grieve a while, then we'll go to work on him and persuade him to let the marshal pursue the matter.'

'I didn't say it was Walt Risby,' hissed Frank, 'but he's got it fixed in his mind that Walt is to blame, and he won't ever let that go.'

'He'll see reason,' insisted Tom.

Frank disagreed. 'What makes you think that? He's convinced that I'm a failure and nothing I do is ever going to change that, so why should Walt expect leniency?'

'Frank!' Tom wanted to tell his brother that he was mistaken but found himself unable to find the necessary words. He, too, was affected by their sister's death and confrontations within the family were the last thing he wanted. Frank had finally shaken off the grip on his sleeve and was following his father towards the house.

Two women stood outside the house, watching the men who were strung out along the route back from the grove. One of the women was Alice Brewster. At her husband's suggestion, the doctor's wife had driven out to prepare Mary for burial. She'd brought along Clara Buxton who had been Mary's closest friend. Ben Hoag's initial reaction to their arrival had been less than hospitable but the lard needed to be washed from his daughter's body before it was clothed in her best dress, and women's hands were needed for such tasks. He relinquished his opposition to their presence at the house but would not permit them to attend the burial process. They were obliged to wait at the house along with the three or four ranch-hands who had gathered in the yard. An awkwardness hung about the men, unsure of what was expected of them. Barring them from the graveside had curtailed a regular display of respect for their boss's daughter, but it didn't seem right to conduct the rough-riding, raucous business of pushing beef. So, they'd hung about the yard, hats removed, watching the activity in the distant grove.

Ben Hoag had almost reached the house when he became aware of the three horsemen coming quickly along the ridge from the north before descending towards the ranch-house. They were yet two hundred yards from his boundary fence when he recognized the leading rider. Immediately, Ben veered towards the gateway, his stride lengthening and quickening, implanting his manner with hostility.

Mort Risby wasn't a big man but his width gave him a square appearance when he was in the saddle that was unmistakeable to those who knew him. He was a heavy, bull-like man whose physical prowess was a source of pride.

He had always believed himself capable of working longer and harder than any man he'd ever hired, and even in his advancing years, was still regarded as the strongest man in the territory. But he wasn't a brutal man and now, as he approached the gateway to the Hoag ranch, he tried to hide any expression of anger. The marshal had told him not to come here but he had never been one for avoiding problems head-on. He'd been angered by Ben's threats against Walt but that had been tempered by the news of Mary Hoag's death. There had been disputes between the men over the years but in Mort's opinion, riding over to the Hoag place was the neighbourly thing to do. Mary's death was a significant loss to the people in this part of Montana. Moreover, it gave Mort the opportunity to put Ben's mind at rest concerning Walt. That was a misconception he couldn't allow to develop. He slowed the pace of his mount to a gentle canter before coming to a halt at the closed gate.

'Ben,' he called, 'Silas Tasker told me about the fire. It's a bad business.'

'Is that all you've got to say?' Ben's voice was heavy with anger.

'Nothing I can say or do that will alter what's happened, Ben.'

'But your boy can turn himself in to the marshal. Face his punishment like a man.'

Mort shook his head slowly. 'Walt didn't have anything to do with what happened here,' he said. 'He's in Miles City. Went there yesterday.'

'Went there last night after he burned my building and killed my daughter.'

'That's not true, Ben. You've got no reason to make such accusations against my son.'

'He was here, Mort. He was seen and recognized. He killed Mary and I mean to see that he hangs for it.'

The bitterness, the certainty in Ben Hoag's denouncement startled Mort Risby. Beside him, Luke Bywater and Steve Tumbrell shifted uneasily in their saddles. Ben Hoag's accusations couldn't be easily ignored. They eyed their boss, unsure how he would react.

'Ben,' Mort said, 'I'm really sorry about what happened to Mary. I figure I know how much you're hurting inside. The Lord knows that nobody had a bad word for her or would have wished her to perish in that manner.'

'You don't know how much I'm hurting, Mort Risby, but you will when they hang your son.'

Mort's face blanched. 'I came here to pay my respects as a good neighbour should, but I refuse to listen to any more of that talk. You're driving a wedge between us, Ben, that could lead to all kinds of trouble.'

'There'll be trouble between us until your boy has paid for what he's done.' With those words uttered, Ben reached towards a saddle that had been slung over the perimeter fence and pulled a rifle free of its boot. Pointing it threateningly, he added, 'Now git.'

Mort pulled on the reins, his horse stepped backwards, away from the gate.

'I'm going,' he said, 'but if you ever pull a gun on me again, you'd better be prepared to use it.'

4

Mary Hoag's death was the talk of Stanton that day, and nowhere was the subject more discussed than in the big trading store which stood apart and dominated the east end of Main Street, much like the newly-built church dominated the west end. The store had been there as long as Stanton had been a town, and had prospered and grown as more and more people settled in the area. Its original owner had quit Montana a year earlier, gone to spend the fortune he'd acquired in San Francisco, Philadelphia, Chicago or New Orleans, depending upon which resident was relaying the information. Gus Hubber had been both cantankerous and querulous, the sort of man who obtained pleasure in causing petty arguments. His replacement, Joe Danvers, was younger, polite and eager to please his customers, but it was Beth Danvers who had the greatest impact on the populace. She, too, was young and had that kind of pleasant disposition that fostered cordiality with almost everyone she met, especially the women, who were eager to glean details of the fashions and lifestyles she brought from the east. Their business flourished and the store, which in Gus Hubber's days had been the haunt of grumbling, checker-playing, idle men, increasingly became a place where women met to exchange gossip, ideas and information.

During the morning, as the news of the tragedy spread, the first reactions of the townspeople of Stanton was an outpouring of shock and sympathy. It wasn't long, however, before those with historical grievances against any member of the Hoag family, threaded trails of comeuppance through the grief. It was the minister's wife who highlighted the hasty, un-Christian funeral that had been performed. Not only had the body not been laid to rest in the town's cemetery, she complained, but her husband who had been ordained for such services, had been ignored. It was a grumble that carried no weight with the older residents who understood Ben Hoag's desire to have his daughter buried alongside her mother, but, influenced by the minister's wife, others were less charitable. Although they couldn't attach a specific reason for their suspicion, they were sure that there was something insidious in the rancher's behaviour.

It was the minister's wife's third visit of the day to the store on Main Street and on this occasion, there was no pretence that she'd come to buy anything.

Cora Hope had seen Alice Brewster return to town in the buggy her husband used for his visits, and had hurried along the street in the hope of learning the latest news from the Hoag ranch. Now, close to the street door, she accosted three townswomen to whom she quietly imparted her sly insinuations of wrong-doing.

From time-to-time, Beth Danvers raised her head from the account book she was studying, and cast a glance in the direction of the group by the door. She could guess their topic of conversation because few people had spoken of anything other than the death of Mary Hoag all day. Living out of town meant that Mary had been an infrequent customer but, even so, Beth had been shocked by the news of her death. In the course of the day, she'd heard the views of most of the Stanton women. Universally, they held a favourable opinion of Mary, but that didn't hold for every member of the Hoag family. Many people in town were irked by Ben's gruff manner, and Tom's introversion belittled him in the eyes of others. It angered Beth that sympathy for the girl's dreadful death had become marred by these instances of unrelated umbrage. She was particularly repulsed by the fact that the minister's wife seemed to be the most vociferous in despoiling the character of the Hoag family, and for no greater reason than that her husband's office had been slighted. Beth didn't approve, but she had a store to run and couldn't banish everyone whose opinion was contrary to her own. If they gossiped in her store then, eventually, they would spend their money here, too. But she still wished that everyone would just mourn Mary's death and forget about the behaviour of the rest of that family.

Once again, Beth raised her head, her attention caught this time by a movement in the doorway. The group of women shuffled aside to give the newcomer access to the interior. He was a slim man in a storebought suit. He wasn't short, but he had a stoop-shouldered gait that made him appear less tall than his near six-feet. He was bareheaded but that was because he'd simply crossed the street from the shop where he cut hair, shaved faces and heated water for the tin tubs that were occasionally occupied by visiting cowboys. He said good-day to Mrs Hope and her companions then made his way to the counter at the back of the store. He seemed interested in every item of stock on display, his eyes scanning the shelves and table layouts he passed, but nothing interrupted his progress. It never did. He always pretended to be surprised to find Beth at whichever counter she was attending, but he'd known her location from the moment he'd entered the store. Jack Temple made Beth Danvers nervous, especially at times like this when Joe wasn't around. She knew that men found her attractive and there were others in town who found it difficult to hide their thoughts when their eyes settled on her, but she always sensed something sinister in Jack's behaviour.

Still, he came into the store as a customer, so she smiled when he reached the counter.

'I'm short of smokes,' he told her. While she was retrieving a pack of his preferred black cigarillos from an under-counter drawer, he spoke again. 'Can't get to sleep at night without some tobacco to relax me.'

Momentarily, Beth paused. The inflection in Jack Temple's voice hinted that his words hid another meaning, one which carried a threat, which somehow gave him a power over her that he meant to use. When she looked up, however, he'd turned away, his attention fixed on the group of women at the other end of the store.

'They, I presume,' he said as he picked up his pack of smokes, 'are discussing the events out at the Hoag place.'

'I imagine so,' Beth replied. 'Little else has been spoken of in here today.'

A sly smile curled the corners of Jack's mouth. 'Must have been a terrible shock for Frank Hoag when he returned home.'

Beth Danvers tried to appear ignorant of Jack Temple's meaning, but she couldn't prevent the colour suddenly draining from her face. Jack gently tossed the pack of smokes in his hand before putting them into a side pocket. 'Sometimes I wake in the middle of the night and stand by my window, watching the sleeping town. Interesting things can sometimes be discovered.' He paused, watched Beth Danvers, waited for her to respond. When she refused to lift her eyes to meet his, he spoke again. 'I'm sure your husband will be eager to hear all the details regarding the Hoag family when he returns.'

Now she did look up and every feeling of apprehension that had gripped her was verified by the other's exultant look. 'When does your husband return?' he asked.

'Tonight,' Beth said quietly.

'How unfortunate for me,' Jack Temple said with a shrug of his shoulders, but Beth knew that that wasn't the end of the matter. 'Still,' he continued, 'I'm sure we'll be able to reach some accommodation over the next few days which will keep the details of certain clandestine meetings from your husband's ears.'

Beth's angry glare was met with a smug smile, then Jack Temple quit the store.

All day, the town had been agog with talk of the tragedy at the Hoag ranch, but it wasn't until darkness had settled over Stanton that the confrontation between Ben Hoag and Mort Risby became known. Mort was still rankled by the reception he'd received when he rode into town. He was accompanied by Luke Bywater and Steve Tumbrell, but their reason for leaving the ranch that night was for nothing more spectacular than a few beers and a game of poker in the River Bend Saloon. All three hitched their mounts outside the saloon but when the two ranch-hands went inside, their boss walked along the street to the post office where he hoped to find Jethro Humbo still at his desk. He was disappointed, the office was in darkness and the door locked.

With a curse of frustration, he retraced his steps. Before he reached the rail where he'd hitched his horse, he heard the hoof beats of two others behind him and felt the eyes of their riders on him as they passed by. He glanced towards them, recognized Chet Taylor and another cowboy from the Hoag ranch and watched as they dismounted outside the River Bend Saloon. Both men eased the girth straps on their animals before heading for the batwing doors.

Chet Taylor touched his hat and muttered, 'Mr Risby,' when they met on the boardwalk outside the saloon. It was an acknowledgement of the rancher's presence that on another occasion he might have deemed unnecessary, but he saw no reason to add to the tension that had been generated earlier in the day. Buck Downs, taking a lead from Chet, touched his hat also before pushing the swing doors aside to gain access to the noisy saloon.

Mort Risby offered a surly reply, a denigration of Ben Hoag who, he said, could learn a lot about basic politeness from his own work-hands.

Chet didn't follow his friend into the saloon. He stopped and faced the owner of the Triple-R ranch. 'Mr Risby,' he began, 'me and Buck have come into town to wash the smoke from our throats, we're not looking for trouble or argument. It's been a bad day out at the ranch and I'm real sorry for what's happened to Mr Hoag and his boys. Perhaps you think he overstepped the mark when you turned up at the ranch earlier, and perhaps he did, but up to now he's been a good boss and he has my loyalty. So, don't bad-mouth him again, Mr Risby. I suggest you give him a wide berth until his grieving's done.'

Irked to be spoken to in such a manner, Mort Risby prepared to respond to Ben Hoag's young foreman. Before he could speak, however, a figure pushed away from the wall and emerged from the shadows.

'That sounds like good advice, Mr Risby,' said Silas Tasker. 'In fact, it sounds like the same advice I gave you this morning. I told you Ben Hoag wanted only his family at the funeral.'

'I went to pay my respects. We've been neighbours for thirty years and I'd known Mary all her life. It was the natural thing to do.'

Silas Tasker motioned his head, a signal for Chet Taylor to join his friend inside the River Bend Saloon. To Mort Risby he said, 'Let's go along to my office and we'll talk about this. What I just over-heard suggests that by interrupting the funeral you made matters worse.'

'The funeral was over before I got there.'

'So, what happened?'

'He pulled a gun on me,' announced Mort. 'Pulled a gun on me and threat-ened to hang my son. No matter how deep his grief, it doesn't give him the right to do those things.'

Silas agreed but he didn't want to charge at the problem like a wounded buffalo. He couldn't help feeling that if Mort Risby had stayed away from Ben Hoag for a couple of days, then Ben Hoag's grief would have subsided and the whole incident could have been investigated in a calm and orderly man-ner. Riding out to the Hoag ranch when he wasn't wanted had only enhanced the involvement of the Risbys in Ben Hoag's troubled mind.

'What are you doing in town?' Silas asked.

'Hoped to catch the telegraph office

open,' the rancher replied. 'Wanted to get a message to Walt in Miles City. It's probably a good idea for him to stay there for a few days. He won't object.'

'Jethro will send a message early in the morning. Do you mean to stay in town tonight?'

Before Mort could supply an answer, gunshots cracked loud, bringing an abrupt end to their conversation. Silas Tasker turned and hurried back towards the River Bend Saloon.

Several customers had been standing at the bar when Chet Taylor and Buck Downs had entered the saloon, but the barman had still slid two glasses of beer to them along the polished counter. Only after both men had drunk deeply did the barman ask for the latest details from the Hoag ranch.

'Nothing to report,' said Chet. He didn't want to speculate on the cause of the fire or the identity of anyone responsible for it. 'Mary's buried. Let that be an end to it.'

Neither Chet nor Buck had noticed

the two Triple-R riders at a nearby table. They were playing penny poker with Jack Temple and Jethro Humbo. Steve Tumbrell and Luke Bywater exchanged a look of incredulity and it was the former who spoke up.

'Don't see how that can be the end of it when your boss is threatening to shoot people without any cause.'

Buck began to turn to answer the Triple-R man, but Chet put a hand on his arm to restrain him. 'Leave it,' he said. There was bad blood between Buck and Steve Tumbrell; it had started over a girl and come to a head when Buck caught Steve cheating in a card game. He was merciless in the ensuing fight, leaving Steve incapable of herding cattle for a week afterwards. Now they tended to avoid each other, and Chet and Buck would have gone elsewhere this night if they'd known the Triple-R man was already in the River Bend Saloon.

'Who'd Ben threaten to shoot?' asked the barman.

'Mr Risby.' That information was supplied by Luke Bywater. He added, 'We went across to the funeral to pay our respects, and old man Hoag pulled a rifle on us. Threatened to shoot us.'

'Is that true?' the barman asked Chet.

'It's a bad time for the boss,' Chet said. 'He'd watched his daughter die. Let it go.'

'Let it go!' exclaimed Steve Tumbrell. 'Don't seem likely that Mr Risby will let it go. Old man Hoag blames Walt for his daughter's death and intends to have him hanged for it.' The silence which descended on the room with those words was broken by the barman's rough tones. 'Blames Walt! Why?'

'Because he's crazy.'

'He's not crazy,' snapped Buck Downs, 'there are reasons.'

'What reasons?' asked Jethro Humbo.

Again, Chet rested a hand on Buck's arm, hoping to put an end to the exchange of words.

'What reasons?' Jethro asked again.

'I reckon the marshal'll sort it out,' Chet said. He drained his glass and nudged Buck's arm for him to do the same. If they intended staying in town, they would do their drinking along the street in the Irishman's bar.

Luke Bywater spoke up. 'I heard Silas Tasker tell Mr Risby that Frank Hoag says he saw Walt hanging around the barn before it went up in flames.'

'Frank Hoag's a liar,' Steve Tumbrell shouted. 'Everyone knows that Walt went off to Miles City yesterday.'

'You watch your mouth, Steve Tumbrell,' Buck said. 'You've called Mr Hoag crazy and Frank a liar. One more insult against the Hoags and you'd better be prepared to back up your words.' He eased the revolver in its holster, not only to emphasise the consequences Steve faced if he didn't desist, but also to ensure that his pistol would come freely away from the leather if that became necessary.

The people in the saloon began to shift to the edges of the room. All eyes were fixed on the two Hoag riders who were still standing against the bar, and

Steve Tumbrell who had kept his place at the card table.

Chet said, 'Take it easy, Buck. Drink up and let's go.'

Buck said nothing. His eyes were fixed on Steve Tumbrell.

Luke Bywater knew that his companion had been seeking an opportunity to get even with Buck ever since he'd taken a beating. Now, with his hands hidden below the table, no one saw him remove his pistol from its holster. Nor did they witness the slight nudge he gave his friend.

The smile that spread across Steve Tumbrell's face surprised everyone in the room. The history between the two men was well known and the knowledge that Buck was the more capable man in any situation was accepted by all. So, the confidence depicted by the stretching smile was difficult to understand. Steve Tumbrell was relaxed, indeed he seemed eager to face the challenge that had been proposed. He lifted his hands above the level of the table so that they could be clearly seen by Buck and Chet.

'All the Hoags are crazy liars,' he said.

Buck's right hand grasped for the Colt in his holster. Before he could raise it, a gun appeared in the other's hand and two bullets smashed into his chest. Buck pitched full-length on the floor and was dead before anyone else moved.

5

Chet Taylor stared at the lifeless figure at his feet, stunned by the death of his friend. He raised his head until his eyes met those of Steve Tumbrell. If he'd entertained thoughts of revenge against Buck's killer, they were instantly abandoned. The gun that fired the lethal shots had been re-cocked and was pointed now at his own chest. Behind it he could see the killer's cold smile of triumph and a glint in his eyes that hinted that he would not be reluctant to pull the trigger again.

'He called it,' said Tumbrell, 'every man here knows that to be true. It was a fair fight but if you see it different then go ahead and make your play.'

For several tense seconds a silence hung over the room. Those men who had quit their tables or their station along the counter, remained unmoving against the walls, watchful of the major players in the affair. It was the barman who first broke the atmosphere, his voice as harsh on his clients' ears as blacksmith's rasp on horseshoes. 'Enough,' he shouted, 'I'll have no more gunplay in here.'

His words still hung in the air when the swing doors were swept open and Silas Tasker stepped into the room. Mort Risby was two steps behind. Both men stopped when they saw the body on the floor.

'What happened here?' Silas asked.

'I guess he wasn't as quick as he thought, marshal.'

Steve Tumbrell's leering reply angered Silas Tasker. 'Give me that gun,' he ordered. 'You're under arrest until I find out what's happened here.'

'He threatened me, and I beat him to the draw. Buck was the aggressor. Everyone here will confirm that.'

A few bystanders nodded their heads or uttered grunts of affirmation, but they didn't deter Silas from doing his duty. He stepped forward, hand outstretched for the weapon that had slain Buck Downs. 'Come with me,' he told Steve Tumbrell, 'you're under arrest while I investigate this killing.'

Tumbrell got to his feet but it was to register protest at the marshal's decision. He saw no reason to be locked up when he was sure that no man present would contradict his assertion that it had been a fair fight. That contradiction, however, was apparent to the marshal as soon as the killer arose and revealed that his holster still contained a pistol.

'Whose gun is this?' Silas asked, as he grasped the still-warm barrel of the gun in Tumbrell's hand.

No one answered immediately but with his confidence dented by the mistake of not returning the gun to its rightful owner, Steve Tumbrell's gaze wandered towards his still-seated companion from the Triple-R ranch.

Silas Tasker addressed the three men who remained sitting around the table. 'Get up.' Jack Temple and Jethro Humbo obeyed immediately. Luke Bywater hesitated until the marshal repeated his command and backed up his words with a motion of the gun he now held. Still, Bywater's reaction was slow, his eyes fixed on the marshal as though he would pounce on him if presented with any opportunity to do so. At first, the murmurs that arose at the sight of his empty holster were low, but they grew and were laden with repugnance when its implication dawned on the men in the room.

It was Chet Taylor who voiced the accusation at Luke Bywater. 'You put that gun in his hand. You ambushed Buck.' Turning his attention to Steve Tumbrell, he added, 'You deliberately goaded him into reaching for his gun to get revenge for the beating he gave you. You planned it together because, on your own you knew you weren't capable of beating him.'

After removing the pistol from Steve Tumbrell's holster, Silas Tasker ordered the pair down to the jail.

'It was murder,' Chet declared as the Triple-R riders were herded towards the saloon door.

Silas told him to wait in the saloon

until he returned. 'I'll hear your version of events after I've locked up these two. Somebody fetch the doctor to certify Buck's death, then have him moved to the undertaker's place.'

Mort Risby wanted to know how long Silas meant to keep his ranch-hands under lock and key. 'This is a busy period,' he protested, 'I can't manage with two men short.'

'Then hire some more,' the marshal told him. 'Seems likely they'll have to stand before a judge and he ain't due in town for a week or two. If the charge is murder, I won't be letting them out of the cells before their trial.'

Mort hadn't expected any other answer, but he still didn't like it. He voiced his objections to an unrelenting marshal all the way to the jail house. The prisoners were put into separate cells and, when he and Mort Risby left the office, Silas took the unusual step of locking the street door, too.

As they retraced their steps, both men were aware of the rowdy noises coming from the River Bend. The place was seldom quiet, but the din rarely rose above the drone of men in idle conversation, mixed with the jangling notes of the barroom piano. Stanton no longer had the reputation of a frontier cattle town and incidents of violence and gunplay were rare. It had been almost three years since the last man had been killed on this street. A peaceful town suited Silas but not only as testimony to his own efficiency as a policeman. If Stanton was ever to become as important as Billings or Butte, then it needed to garner the renown of a civilised town in order to attract more settlers and businesses to the area.

For now, though, the ruckus in the saloon was of secondary importance to the marshal. Four men were carrying Buck Downs' body on a plank along the street towards Noah Pink's timber-yard where the coffins were made. Abe Brewster trailed behind. He was jacketless and hatless, indicating the alacrity with which he'd responded to the call for his services, but stopped when he recognized the figures who were heading his way.

'What's going on around here?' he asked, the question was almost a grumble and it was clear that he didn't expect either the marshal or the rancher to provide an answer. 'Two good people wiped away from the world unnecessarily. In my experience, people die easily enough without the need of help from anyone else.' He threw a look at Mort Risby that almost held an accusation, but he began walking again without another word.

'You'll give me a note to certify Buck's death?' Silas asked.

'I'll bring it in the morning,' Abe threw over his shoulder. Then he stopped and turned to face the others. 'Two gunshot wounds, either of which would have killed him. Close together, like the shooter had time to take careful aim before pulling the trigger.'

'What are you implying, Doctor?' asked Mort Risby.

'I'm not implying anything,' Abe

replied. 'Just telling you what I'll tell the judge when your men stand trial.'

'My men!' reiterated Mort Risby pointedly. 'Steve Tumbrell's quarrel with Buck Downs was a private matter. It had nothing to do with me or the Triple-R.'

Silas Tasker was surprised by Abe Brewster's remark. Inflaming arguments wasn't the doctor's normal practice. He gave voice to that opinion.

'It's not me you need to be talking to,' Abe told him. 'A lot of things have been said back there and there's a swell of feeling against you and yours, Mr Risby.'

The marshal looked up the street, the noise emanating from the River Bend now a source of concern. He could hear the barman bellowing. Although his actual words didn't carry to the three men on the street, his meaning was clear. He was attempting to establish some semblance of order within the saloon.

His anger rising, Mort Risby demanded an explanation from the doctor for his words.

'People are putting two and two

together,' Abe said. 'There was already sympathy for the Hoags over Mary's death, and common rumour has your son involved in that.'

Mort Risby snapped at him. 'The Triple-R wasn't involved in the fire that killed Mary Hoag.'

'Perhaps not, but what's now seen as the coldblooded killing of Buck Downs by two of your men has got people talking about a feud between your spread and the Diamond-H. Some people think a range war is brewing.'

At that moment, a yell followed by more loud shouts and the sounds of breaking furniture carried along the street from the direction of the River Bend. The doctor cursed, wondered aloud if he was to get any rest that day, then followed in the wake of Silas Tasker who was already hurrying to investigate the commotion.

Two townsmen were hurrying outside as the marshal approached the swing doors. Recognizing Silas, one of the men informed him of the identity of the brawlers. 'It's Chet Taylor and Jack Temple,' he said, before hurrying away from the vicinity with his companion.

Silas peered into the room. Once again, the customers were lining the walls but this time they'd vacated the tables and their places at the counter, not to get out of the line of fire, but to give room to the combatants who were scuffling amidst overturned tables and broken glasses. The barman, who had come from behind the bar with a stout club in his hand, was yelling at them to stop or take the quarrel outside, but his words were having no effect. It was clear that he was willing to crack either or both skulls but because they were rolling and hauling each other around the room, was unable to deliver any kind of telling blow. It was also apparent to Silas that, as expected when he heard the names of those involved, Chet Taylor had the upper hand.

With both hands, Jack Temple was gripping Chet's shirt front, keeping close to his opponent so that the ranch-hand's punches couldn't be delivered with a full swing of the arm. Previous blows, however, had found their mark. His face was marked, and blood was flowing freely from cuts, both above and below his left eye. He was in pain and breathing raggedly through his mouth and when Chet attempted to twist himself free of his hold, Jack's draining resistance became apparent to everyone in the room. His knees buckled, and he would have gone to the floor if not for his stubborn hold on his adversary's shirt.

Silas drew his pistol and fired two shots into the night sky before stepping into the saloon. The gunfire had an effect on those watching the fight, especially the men nearest the door who stepped aside to make a pathway through to the middle of the room, but it didn't put an end to the struggle; something more than remote gunshots was needed to distract the combatants from their purpose.

'That's enough,' Silas shouted as he grabbed the back of Chet Taylor's shirt collar and hauled him backwards. Pitting his own strength against the waning energy of the fighters, he pushed his body between them. 'Enough,' he yelled again.

His wasn't the only voice that could be heard. 'You'll pay for this damage,' the barman shouted. 'Next time you want to brawl, do it out on the street.' To emphasise his point, he smacked the cudgel across Chet's shoulders. The Diamond-H rider staggered forward and collided with Silas Tasker who was trying to lug Jack Temple onto one of the few nearby seats that were still upright.

'Get back behind the counter, Bart,' the marshal told the barman, 'and you,' he said to Chet Taylor, 'sit down there because if you bump into me again I'll charge you with assaulting a peace officer.'

Slowly, the glare of animosity that Chet had fixed on Jack Temple began to subside. It wasn't that he had lost his bitterness for the barber, but with much of his energy spent and his shoulders sore from the blow from Bart Martin's baton, he knew he was no match for the marshal.

'Somebody want to tell me what's going on here?' asked Silas.

Chet pointed an accusing finger at Jack Temple.

'He was part of the plot to kill Buck,' he said.

'I was not,' responded the other.

'You were at the table with them. You must have seen Luke Bywater pass his gun to Steve Tumbrell.'

Wiping away the blood that was running into his left eye, Jack Temple denied that accusation too.

'But you agree with them about Mr Hoag and his family. You think they are liars.'

'Marshal!' A voice from among the spectators interrupted proceedings. A tall, fair-haired man stepped forward. 'Perhaps I can explain. I think it was something I said which sparked the fury.'

'Go ahead, Mr Danvers. Say what you've got to say.'

'I got here after the shooting. In fact,

I came to see what had happened. There was a lot of talking linking the fire out at the Hoag place with the gunfight and the prospect of a feud between the Triple-R and the Diamond-H. An argument started up about the whereabouts of Walt Risby when the fire that killed Mary Hoag was started. Well, I've just returned from Miles City, been there on business for a couple of days, and I mentioned that I hadn't bumped into young Walt while I was there.'

'Miles City is a bigger place than Stanton,' snapped Mort Risby. 'Just because you didn't see him doesn't mean he wasn't there.'

Joe Danvers held out his hands in a placatory gesture. 'I agree, but it seemed to be sufficient proof for some people that your son had been hanging around the Diamond-H last night.'

The marshal cast a look at Chet Taylor, wondering if he had been the ringleader of such an attitude.

'In fairness,' Joe Danvers said, reading the marshal's suspicion, 'Chet was avoiding involvement in the conversation until Jack sprang to Walt's defence and said that there was no proof that Frank Hoag was telling the truth.'

After the events of the past few hours, Silas Tasker could understand why that would anger Chet. The expression of similar sentiments had cost the life of his companion. He would be burning inside for some kind of justice for the slaying of Buck Downs.

'Chet,' he said, 'get back to the ranch. I'll be there early in the morning to talk to Mr Hoag and get your version of events.'

Without a word, Chet gathered up his hat which had come adrift during the scuffle, then went outside, climbed into the saddle and leading the bronc that Buck had ridden into town, lit out for the Diamond-H.

While Abe Brewster attended to the abrasions sustained by Jack Temple during his fight with Chet Taylor, Silas spoke to those customers who had been present when Buck Downs was killed. It soon became clear that no one had seen

Luke Bywater pass his gun under the table, but most were agreed that there was no other explanation for Steve Tumbrell's success. The gun had appeared in his hand before Buck Downs had begun to draw his own revolver. No one could point to anything in his past that marked the Triple-R rider as a quick-draw artist but they all agreed that he had baited Buck Downs with a gloating certainty of success. When Silas Tasker left the River Bend, he knew the charges against Steve Tumbrell and Luke Bywater would be murder.

6

Working long hours and battling weariness while planning the next day's chores was commonplace for Tom Hoag. Although Ben Hoag was still the boss of the outfit, he'd been eased aside by his eldest son when it came to the day-to-day running of the ranch. Tom's instinct for the cattle business had developed into natural leadership and it was from him that the men received their orders each morning and to whom they reported at the end of shift. It wasn't unusual for him to be in the yard after dark, issuing instructions to the riders for the following day or checking the animals in the corrals and stables. This night, however, he was in the yard alone, arms resting on the top rail of the boundary fence while he gazed at the dark mounds of rising land which led off to the Dearborn and beyond.

He'd spoken with the men in the

bunkhouse earlier, had tried to maintain a semblance of normality to the allotment of tasks and duties, but it hadn't been easy. Even the toughest of the hired men were affected by Mary's death and orders had been accepted without any of the grumbles or boisterous jocularity that habitually marked occasions when men of their ilk gathered together. Those who had been given night-duties had gathered their equipment as though eager to get away from the ranch. In contrast, Chet and Buck who had expressed a need for a glass of beer in Stanton, had shown a strange reluctance to saddle-up and leave the ranch behind. No one else had plans to leave the bunkhouse that night.

Tom couldn't rightly explain his own feelings as he smoked a quirly in the cooling darkness. Anger predominated. It hung like an extra layer over the heavy cloak of sadness that smothered him. It disrupted his ability to think clearly and wouldn't allow him to rest his mind with sleep. The source of his anger was his own family. Frank had barely spoken two words since the last shovelful of soil had been thrown over their sister, but their father had relentlessly spilt words of vengeance for the death of his favourite child. At first, Tom had attempted to appease his father, to reason with him that there was no proof that Walt Risby was guilty of starting the fire, but he soon relinquished the attempt. His words were harshly brushed aside by his father, and appealing for Frank's support was worthless. The pre-existing squabbles between that son and his father had been further aggravated by his absence from the ranch at the time of the fire so his meanly-stated assertions that he couldn't positively identify Walt Risby were without conviction. Tom thought his brother was more afraid of increasing his father's wrath against him than telling the truth. Ben seemed more inclined to believe that his youngest son's uncertainty was another pointer to the weakness of his character, that he lacked the courage to provide the evidence that would hang

Walt Risby. Frank had gone to his room to hide from his father while his father had gone to his office to feed his curses and threats with liquor from a whiskey bottle.

It meant that the task of running the ranch had fallen squarely on Tom's shoulders. Perhaps, in the morning, his father would resume his role as head of the family, but for now, responsibility for the ranch was all Tom's and he couldn't decide if that added to his anger or kept it in check. He'd spoken calmly to the ranch-hands, hoping to eliminate any influence transmitted by his father's wild accusations; he neither wanted to lose men who, wary of a coming range war, might ride away, nor did he wish to arouse a militant spirit in others and risk the animosity of the Stanton townspeople. As it was, if his father's words and behaviour were spread abroad, there would be little goodwill extended to the Hoag family. Any sympathy the populace had for the loss of Mary would soon disappear if lead began flying and men were killed and injured.

It was as he stood with his back resolutely turned to the charred timbers of the barn, as though looking upon them would be an affront to the memory of his sister, that he picked up the figure of the horseman approaching from the direction of Stanton. He was slow to recognize Chet Taylor because his baffled mind was trying to make sense of an earlier incident that had been sparked by his father's ill-mannered demeanour. Pleasantries had never come easily to Ben Hoag's lips but as he seldom mixed in town society, his ill-grace was noted but rarely gave offence. Around the ranch, the men accepted his surliness because pushing cows was a tough business, and he paid their wages, but that afternoon, his behaviour had been inexcusable despite the extenuating circumstances of his daughter's death. The confrontation with Mort Risby had been deplorable, but that had been a clash between two bullish men who had locked horns in the past and for whom disputes were the spices that seasoned the meal of life. Mrs Brewster and Clara Buxton, however, had turned up at the ranch to help the family in its time of need and had not deserved the rough words and brusque manners with which they were greeted and eventually dismissed from the Diamond-H.

As he'd helped the women into the doctor's buggy, Tom had spoken words of apology. It had been difficult for Mrs Brewster to hide her annoyance. She had taken up the reins with the clear intention of leaving the Diamond-H as swiftly as possible. Clara Buxton, however, had dawdled a moment while she adjusted her bonnet before climbing up beside her companion. As she raised her head, she also reached out and rested a hand on Tom's arm. Her brown eyes looked into his own and held his attention before she spoke.

'You're always welcome at the farm, Tom,' she told him. 'Come by any time.'

The invitation had surprised Tom. Other than a greeting when they encountered each other in Stanton, he had rarely spoken to Clara. The demands of running a ranch sent him hither and thither across the range land so that he had seldom been around the ranch-house when his sister's friend had come to visit, and only once had he been to Clem Buxton's farm. He hadn't set eyes on Clara that day, had stopped only long enough for Mary to clamber down from the wagon before slapping the reins and urging the team on to Stanton. But none of that meant that he was unaware of Clara Buxton. He could understand how she and his sister had become close friends, because they seemed to share a similar attitude to life. Mary had been able to find pleasure in every situation and a smile was never far from her lips. Likewise, a smile always lit up Clara's face when he encountered her in Stanton. There had been occasions when she'd seemed prepared to engage him in conversation, but he'd always evaded those moments. He told himself he had neither the aptitude nor the leisure for idle chit-chat. Whatever errand had brought him to town needed to be completed as swiftly as possible so that he could return to the jobs that required his attention at the Diamond-H.

Tom had never managed to adopt that easy manner around women, that came so easily to men like Walt Risby. Even his younger brother, Frank, was ever eager to ride into Stanton to attend the regular Saturday night dance at the Meeting Room and, indeed, to be high stepping with Lily Cregar's girls at the cruder assemblies in the River Bend. It wasn't Tom's way. The prosperity of the ranch was always uppermost in his mind and he shunned anything that might interfere with that goal. Still, as he leant against the yard rails, the picture in his mind was that of Clara Buxton's face, a memory of her turning to look at him as Mrs Brewster drove the buggy through the gate and up the small rise that led onto the trail to Stanton. Her large, dark eyes were fixed on his, and despite the solemnity of the occasion, he thought a smile was trying to stretch her lips. Tom was still considering its meaning when his recollection of the departing buggy was interrupted by the new arrival. It took a moment to assemble the knowledge that there were two horses but only one rider.

'Where's Buck?' he called as Chet rode into the yard. 'What's happened?'

Chet waited until he was inside the ranch-house to relate the full story. Tom Hoag listened with growing incredulity. The dispute between Buck and Steve Tumbrell was common knowledge, but he hadn't expected it to end in such a violent manner. There had been disputes, arguments and fights among the cowboys in the past and some had stretched into long-running hostilities, but it was a long time since such a flare-up in Stanton had led to a killing.

'And Marshal Tasker has both Tumbrell and Bywater in jail,' said Tom, his words seeking to confirm what Chet had said.

'That's right. He told Mr Risby that

if they faced a charge of murder, they would be there until the judge arrived for their trial.'

'Mort Risby! He was there?' The angry words came from Ben Hoag whom Tom had summoned to listen to Chet's report.

'Sure was, Mr Hoag. Rode into town with his men.'

Ben Hoag cursed. 'Then he's behind the plot,' he added.

'Pa!' Tom interrupted his father, didn't want him to say anything in front of Chet that might incite the ranch-hands.

Chet Taylor, however, was already shaking his head to deny Ben Hoag's accusation. 'Mr Risby wasn't in the River Bend when the shooting began,' he said. 'Reckon he was with the marshal, least-ways, they arrived together.'

Ben Hoag swept an arm across his body as though pushing away his work-er's words. 'Setting up an alibi,' he stated. 'Making sure that he didn't get jailed with the men he'd paid to do the killing.'

'Pa!' Tom butted in again, 'what reason could Mr Risby have for killing Buck?'

'You heard Chet,' growled his father, 'he's setting the town against this family.'

Tom wanted to argue but Chet was first to speak. This time his words were delivered slowly, with deliberation, as though his opinion was changing in favour of the elder Hoag. 'Sure were some unkind things said against you, Mr Hoag, and some of them said after Tumbrell and Bywater were locked in the calaboose.' He fingered the soft, discoloured mark below his right eye. 'Didn't expect the barber to pick a side.'

'What's he got against this family?' asked Tom.

'Young Frank was his target,' Chet answered.

'He was probably just saying what he'd been paid to say,' Ben growled, 'but it shows how determined Mort Risby is to turn the town against us.' Chet remembered he had a message to deliver. 'Marshal Tasker's coming out here tomorrow.'

'Then he'll get the same reception I gave Mort Risby,' said Ben Hoag. 'He has no authority out here. This is my land, and nobody is taking it without a fight.'

If Tom adjudged his father's comment as unjustified, he chose not to argue against it for the moment. Words that were the product of whiskey-soaked grief might not be repeated in the light of a new day. In the morning he would try to reason with him and help to put an end to the growing tension before the marshal arrived.

★ ★ ★

Tom's hope that sleep would have a pacifying effect on his father's temperament gained no encouragement when he tried to discuss the previous day's events next morning and was completely shattered the moment Silas Tasker hove into view on the western ridge. Ben Hoag, rifle in hand, strode across the yard and closed the yard-gate to emphasise the point that the lawman was not welcome at the ranch. While he waited for the marshal to reach the gate, he was joined by his sons, both of whom were anxious to overhear the up-coming conversation.

Silas reined in his mount and greeted the rancher as though undeterred by the barrier and armed reception. 'Ben,' he said by way of a greeting, 'reckon I speak for most people in Stanton when I say that Mary will be a sore miss in our lives.'

'Yeah! And what are you doing to catch her killer?'

Silas eased himself in the saddle, rested his hands on the pommel-horn and leant forward. 'That's why I'm here, Ben. To investigate what happened. Hear your complaint and have a look around the ruins.'

'You've got no authority out here,' Ben told him.

'You're right, Ben, but what happened in the River Bend last night is my concern and people in town seem to be linking Buck Downs' death with the burning of your barn. I don't want the matter escalating out of control with riders of rival ranches exchanging gunfire in town. We need to get this situation sorted out. I'm here to talk.'

He motioned his head towards the gate, expected it would be opened for him as it always had been on previous visits. The Hoags had never lacked common-place courtesy. Water for his horse and place in the shade for himself had always been his reward following a dusty ride from town; Mary had always brought coffee and biscuits and a welcoming smile while he discussed with her father the business that had brought him to the ranch. But this morning the gate remained closed.

'You can talk from there,' Ben told him.

The rancher's obstinate attitude made Silas uneasy, but he tried not to let it show. Losing his own temper wouldn't help anyone. 'Mort Risby tells me his son was in Miles City at the time of the fire and I've sent a telegraph message to Sheriff Brown asking him to confirm that the lad was there two nights ago. Until I get that reply, I don't want to hear any more accusations or threats against him.'

'Of course, you don't. I've heard that

Mort Risby was your constant companion last night. No doubt you've already dropped the charges against those men who murdered Buck Downs. He's always been jealous of my rich grazing-land and now he's got you in his pocket to help him grab it.'

Silas Tasker bristled at the accusation. 'I'm not in anyone's pocket, Ben, and for your information, Steve Tumbrell and Luke Bywater are still in my cells and they'll remain there until they go on trial to face a charge of murder.' He paused a moment, hoping to detect something in the rancher's stance that would indicate an abatement of his aggressive attitude. When nothing showed, he focussed on Ben's accusation that Mort Risby was trying to steal the Diamond-H's grazing-land. 'What makes you think Mort Risby is trying to encroach on your land?' he asked.

'Because he wants a quicker route to the corrals at the Billings railhead and I won't let him drive his beeves through the Musselshell Valley.'

Silas knew that the route to Billings had previously been a bone of contention between the two ranchers but had thought it an argument long ago resolved. When he saw the look that the brothers exchanged behind their father's back, it seemed clear that they, too, were surprised that such a topic had been revived. Still, they didn't contradict him, so it was left to Silas to give voice to the fact that he hadn't heard anyone, including Mort Risby, mention that such a dispute still existed.

'That's why he wanted Walt to marry my Mary,' Ben Hoag insisted. 'I expect he thought the marriage would allow him access to the valley.'

Again, the brothers seemed uneasy with their father's comments, as though his normal, reasoned behaviour had been derailed by the horrific event that had culminated in their sister's death.

'When I made it clear that my daughter would never be allowed to marry that hellion, they took their revenge by trying to destroy my livestock, but killed my daughter instead.'

Silas said, 'There is no evidence to indicate that Walt had any involvement in starting the blaze that burned down your property. If any is found, then he too will be arrested and put on trial.'

'Of course, there is evidence,' stormed Ben Hoag. 'My boy here,' he indicated Frank who was two steps behind his left shoulder, 'saw him riding away and chased him to the Dearborn.'

'Is that true, Frank?' asked the marshal. 'Can you positively identify Walt Risby?'

Frank shuffled. 'It was dark. I saw the white tail of a horse.'

'Hardly sufficient evidence on which to accuse Walt of any involvement in the crime,' responded the marshal.

'He followed him all the way to the Dearborn,' snarled Ben Hoag, 'all the way to the road that leads to Miles City. You might get an answer to your message that tells you that Walt Risby is currently in Miles City, but he wasn't there when the fire was started. He was here. He killed my daughter and he'll pay for it.'

7

Silas Tasker's request for information from Sheriff Brown concerning the location of Walt Risby wasn't the only telegraphic message that had passed between Stanton and Miles City that morning; Mort Risby had sent one to his son advising him to stay away from home until he was contacted again. That message, however, was never delivered; Walt had already left his hotel with the expectation of reaching the Triple-R long before nightfall.

He was in a buoyant mood as he made the journey home; not only had the business he'd been sent to conduct at the Cattlemen's Bank been trouble-free, but for two nights he'd enjoyed all the pleasures available in a larger settlement and had had his appetite whetted for travel beyond the boundaries of Montana. He wanted to discover if the tales he'd heard about the boisterous towns such as Cheyenne and Abilene were true or if the carnal pleasures available in the great cities, Chicago, St. Louis and Santa Fe, matched his expectations. Jimmy Carson could be persuaded to travel with him; Jimmy had no especial desire to spend the remainder of his days working in the lumber-yard on the edge of town and was as keen on finding fun and adventure as Walt himself.

Thinking of Jimmy jogged the memory of their recent escapade and caused him to chuckle as he rode towards home. They'd gone up into the high ground to swim in a pool they knew that was permanently refreshed with cool water off the hillside. When they got around to talking about the approaching town social, it transpired that they each had the same partner in mind; Esther Hope, the minister's daughter. The result was a race back to town to be the first to pay their addresses to the girl. Walt had pushed Jimmy in the pool, which gave him the edge on reaching the horses first then, in high spirits, he'd chased away

Jimmy's mount to ensure the advantage and be first back to town.

Yipping away the horse wasn't anything Jimmy wouldn't have done to him if the roles had been reversed. Playing tricks on each other had become common-place in their friendship without arousing anger or resentment in either. On this occasion, however, accidently, the inconvenience caused to Jimmy Carson had been greater than intended. If the chestnut gelding had been Jimmy's own horse it wouldn't have run more than a quarter of a mile before pausing to crop grass and await its rider, but Jimmy had hired a livery horse that day and it hadn't stopped running until it got back to the stable in Stanton. Jimmy cursed his friend all the way home, but any rancour he harboured against Walt had disappeared the next day.

It was the gossiping people of Stanton who turned the misfiring escapade into a feat of wilful evil. They, it was, who attached the danger of capture and death at the hands of raiding Arapaho to the discomfort of a long walk home. Both Walt and Jimmy had laughed at that. Perhaps a heifer had been stolen from a remote farm by a hungry warrior, but the possibility of raiding war parties was as likely as driving a wagon over the Bitterroots in winter. These were civilized times; tribal wars were at an end.

Esther Hope had agreed to attend the social with Walt and she was the reason he was hurrying back to the Triple-R. In the wake of the gossip that had branded him with the desertion of his friend, her parents had tried to dissuade her from going through with the undertaking, but she had refused to abandon the plan. It was a source of wonder to Walt that two such sour-faced people as the minister and his wife, could have produced such a pretty and cheerful child and he wondered what God they worshipped who insisted upon the life of permanent misery that seemed to be theirs. To prevent such an existence becoming Esther's fate, he intended to add to her usual cheerfulness by dancing her off her feet.

On reflection, he decided, the Hopes weren't the only people in Stanton whom happiness had apparently passed by. People sneered or objected to every little jape whether they were affected by it or not. It seemed that the young were only worthy of consideration if they worked from dawn 'til dusk and were permitted to smile if following an example set by their elders. He'd never wittingly harmed anyone, never intended any offence but there were countless people in Stanton who gave him a wide berth.

The thought occurred to him that most of the people who disliked him were the fathers of the prettiest girls in town. Even Ben Hoag had been riled at the sight of him talking to Mary. He liked Mary Hoag, who seemed to regard his reputation as the Lothario of Stanton with as much humour as he did himself. She seldom attended the town socials, too busy at the Diamond-H, he supposed, but one day, he promised himself, they would dance together.

It was with his mind full of pleasant

thoughts about pretty girls that Walt reached the point where the trail crossed the Dearborn. As he cantered down to the river's edge, he detected an awkwardness in the horse's gait, so climbed down to inspect the rear leg that seemed to be the cause of the animal's discomfort. The white stallion swished its tail with impatience while Walt inspected its leg for cuts or abrasions then, finding none, lifted its foot off the ground. A small stone had become lodged between hoof and shoe and it needed only a moment for Walt to hook it clear with the aid of his pocket-knife. The stone had provided a bit of leverage to separate the shoe from the hoof, slackening it slightly so that Walt knew he would have to proceed at a gentler pace in order to protect the animal from further discomfort and injury. He allowed it to stand in the cool water for a few moments in the hope that it would heal any remaining soreness.

Across the river, shielded by tall trees littering the high bank that rose to a plateau of open range-land, Walt Risby's ministrations to his troubled animal were observed by two pairs of eyes.

'Should we tell Mr Hoag?' The speaker was Pete Simms who'd been in the yard earlier that day when the boss had defied the marshal and asserted that Walt Risby was responsible for the death of his daughter and would be made to pay for it. The marshal, however, had been adamant that when evidence was produced to prove the young man's guilt, he would be arrested but, until then, anyone who took matters into their own hands would, themselves, face the full power of the law. Pete Simms was unsure if his duty was to Ben Hoag or the law.

The doubts in the mind of Pete's companion were less pronounced. Don Glasco was an older man and had worked at the Diamond-H for several years. Ranch owners were their own law-makers and he had never had cause to doubt Ben Hoag's past decisions. He was reluctant to start now. Still, Ben's behaviour that morning had been unusual, as though he had been gripped with so great a need for vengeance that only a range war would assuage his inner clamour.

'I'll keep an eye on young Risby,' he said. 'You ride back to the ranch. But Pete,' he said before the other put spur to his horse's flanks, 'report to Tom. Let him decide what Mr Hoag should know.'

Pete Simms saw the sense in that course of action and nodded his agreement before speeding off towards the Diamond-H. Half-an-hour later he galloped through the yard-gate and slithered to a halt outside the cookhouse where Matty Slade was rinsing pans under the pump. The cook swatted away the dust stirred up by the animal's abrupt stop.

'Hey!' he shouted. 'If these pots need rewashing, then you're doing them. What's got under your saddle?'

'I'm looking for Tom. Is he around the yard?'

Matty Slade shook his head. 'Saw him ride out an hour ago. No doubt he'll be back when I put some grub on the table.'

Pete looked around as though hoping

the cook was mistaken and the boss's son would come striding across the compound to hear his report. 'Do you know where he went?' he asked.

Matty shook his head and turned his attention back to the pots. 'Went up the trail towards town but I ain't saying that's where he's gone.'

'And you don't know when he'll be back.'

It was difficult to tell if Pete's words were a question or a statement but in either case, they failed to elicit a response from the cook. Instead, a voice, gruff and trouble-laden, growled behind him.

'Don't know when who's coming back?' demanded Ben Hoag.

'I was looking for Tom,' Pete replied.

'Why do you want him?'

Pete hesitated a moment. 'I've got a message for him from Don.'

Ben fixed his eyes on the rider, glowering, as though a message for his son this day was a measure of disrespect to him. 'Spit it out,' he said. 'I'm still the boss of this outfit.'

Again, Pete paused, his tongue licking across dry lips as though needing to wet them before being able to continue.

'Well!' Ben Hoag voiced a surly impatience. 'What's the trouble? Where are you working?'

'Me and Don were working the south range, Mr Hoag. Rounding up strays on the open land near the river.'

'OK. So why aren't you still out there?'

'Don thought Tom should know what we'd seen,' he said. His reluctance to reveal the message to anyone but the man he'd been sent to deliver it to was apparent in the slow manner that the words left his mouth. He shuffled in the saddle.

'What's the matter with you?' snapped Ben Hoag, annoyance mixing with impatience in his tone. It caused Matty Slade to cease his work with the pans and flash a look at Pete Simms, a look which advised him against holding out on the boss, urging him to appease Ben Hoag's growing temper.

'We saw Walt Risby,' said Pete. 'He was

at the crossing point on the Dearborn.'

'Heading which way?' Ben's low voice was full of threat.

'Heading for home, I guess.'

'Get my horse,' shouted Ben, 'and gather the men together. If we hurry, we'll catch him while he's still on the open range.'

'He's not travelling fast,' Pete said. 'I think his horse is lame.'

Ben nodded, a sign of satisfaction that revenge for Mary's death was close at hand.

Matty Slade, who had been at the Diamond-H longer than any of the other hands, tried to dissuade his employer from his intended action. 'Leave it to Marshal Tasker, Mr Hoag. He'll find the evidence to prove young Risby guilty, if he burned down the stable.'

'If!' Ben Hoag roared the one word, his face dark with rage. 'Walt Risby is guilty of killing my daughter. I've doled out punishments to those who've wronged me in the past. I didn't need Silas Tasker or any lawman then and I don't need them now. If you don't want to ride with me then you stay here and cook up a big pan of stew, but ring that bell now and tell the rest of the men to get armed and mounted because I'm not letting Walt Risby see another sundown.'

Four men rode away from the Diamond-H ranch alongside Ben Hoag and Pete Simms. Any personal belief they might have had with regards to the guilt or innocence of Walt Risby was set aside. Mary Hoag's father had suffered a loss for which he sought revenge and the thirty dollars a month he paid for pushing cattle also bought their loyalty. They were armed with rifles in saddle-boots in addition to the pistols that were holstered against their thighs. They clattered out of the yard, the horses put to a steady run as they climbed the first of the low mounds that pointed the way to the Dearborn River.

Frank Hoag opened the ranch-house door and watched the group until it disappeared. Hoping to avoid his father, Frank had remained indoors since the departure of Silas Tasker. Sounds of frantic activity in the yard, however, had aroused his interest, had drawn him outside to investigate. He crossed the compound to find out the cause of the matter from the one person who had remained behind.

'You've got to stop your pa, Frank,' Matty Slade told him after informing him of the news Pete Simms had brought to the ranch. 'If anything happens to Walt Risby, there's a danger of this blowing up into a full-scale range war.'

'Was Tom riding with them?'

'Nobody knows where your brother is, but you haven't got time to worry about that. Get saddled up and catch up to them before they find young Risby. You've got to persuade your father to leave the matter to Marshal Tasker.'

'My father doesn't listen to anything I say except to find fault with it.'

Matty spoke angrily. 'Quit feeling sorry for yourself. A young man's life is in danger. Even if he did start the fire I doubt if he meant for your sister to die.'

Frank was more aware than anyone that suspicion of Walt Risby's involvement had been brought about by his own false testimony and that probably the only way to deflect his father from his purpose was to confess to the fact that he wasn't anywhere near the ranch when the stable went up in flames. It was a course of action that he anticipated with trepidation. He would be despised by everyone in the territory. His father, he supposed, would disown him but his conscience told him that it wasn't right to stand by and see a man persecuted for something he hadn't done. When, once more, Matty Slade urged him to go after the others, he headed for the corral, saddled a mount then galloped away towards the Dearborn crossing.

★ ★ ★

The damage to the white stallion's hoof wasn't critical, it would heal with the application of a salve and a few idle days in the pasture, but once across the river there were still twenty miles to cover to reach the Triple-R ranch. Accordingly, Walt Risby asked no more of the animal than a walking pace and, for long stretches, walked at its head rather than sat astride its back. For the most part, the terrain was suitable walking country. There were occasional low mounds to scale and descend but it was good grass land, unlike the more rugged and rocky country to the west. Still, he would have preferred to ride; there weren't many cowboys who didn't like to be in the saddle.

The thought flicked through his mind that it would brighten Jimmy Carson's day if he happened upon him at this moment. Who would blame his friend if, in such a circumstance, he simply laughed, uttered some comment about marauding Arapaho, then rode away. Of course, he knew that Jimmy wouldn't do that. They'd ride double into Stanton where Walt could hire a livery horse that would take him home. He smiled, his feet were going to be sore when he stood up with Esther Hope at tomorrow night's social.

It was at that moment that he realized he was under observation by horsemen in a line along the brow of a nearby mound. Encountering other riders wasn't to be unexpected. Although Montana was sparsely populated, this was still the main route from the northern territories to the Wyoming border. Also, this was open range land, free grazing for the stock of several of the local ranches.

Walt counted seven riders, too many, he suspected, to be hands from one ranch, especially as he hadn't seen any sign of a herd since crossing the Dearborn. But one by one, in a line, they descended the rise and headed in his direction. Perhaps, he thought, there was a chance he'd be able to ride double with one of these men back to town. That chance, however, diminished when he recognized the leading rider. Ben Hoag's face bore an expression no less severe than when he'd last seen it in Stanton two days earlier. He stopped walking as the riders drew near and studied the six dour faces that looked down at him from their saddles. They'd formed an uneven semi-circle, effectively barring him from moving forward. Walt hadn't expected a friendly greeting from Ben Hoag, but he hadn't expected his own smile to be met with such a sombre response from the others. He knew all the riders; Pete Simms, Chet Taylor and Biff Clayton weren't much older than himself while Don Glasco, Harvey Jacks and the man he knew only as Omaha, had been around the territory as long as he could remember. He had chatted, drunk and gambled with them in the Stanton saloons and squatted around campfires or rode alongside them while checking out the brands on open-range strays.

'Picked up a stone down by the river,' he explained, rubbing the white stallion's long face in a friendly fashion. 'Must have walked four miles already and still got a distance to go.' When the Diamond-H crew remained silent he spoke again. 'Don't suppose you've got a spare mount nearby that I can ride into Stanton.' Walt smiled again.

There was no trace of humour in Ben Hoag's reply. 'That white will get you as far as you're going.'

Walt twisted an unconvincing smile. He knew there was a hidden meaning in the rancher's words, but he couldn't figure out what it could be. He addressed his next remark to Chet Taylor whose extravagant manner of high-stepping girls around a dance-floor was a reflection of the joy afforded by the activity. 'If I have to walk all the way to Stanton I reckon I'll be no more capable of dancing at tomorrow's social than that wooden Indian outside the Danvers' store.'

'I reckon you'll do your next jig just fine,' Ben Hoag told him. 'Biff, throw your rope over him.'

'Hey!' Walt shouted. 'What's going on here? What's this all about?' As he spoke he stepped to the other side of his horse, putting it between himself and the owner of the Diamond-H but aware that Biff Clayton, if he unstrung his rope, would be no less capable of flipping it over his head.

'It's about the death of my daughter,' Ben Hoag told him. 'You've got to pay for that.'

'Mary. Mary's dead?'

'She died in agony. Killed by the fire you started.'

'Fire! I didn't start any fire.'

'You were seen, betrayed by your white horse. Fitting that its injury has allowed you to fall into our hands.'

'You've got this wrong, Mr Hoag. I haven't done anything to cause Mary's death. I left for Miles City shortly after I spoke to you in Stanton. There are people there who can verify that.'

'And there are people here who saw you riding away from our ranch towards the Dearborn shortly before the fire was discovered. Biff, what are you waiting for?'

Biff Clayton had his rope uncoiled but had delayed spinning the loop until the talking was done. Walt Risby's surprise at the news of Mary Hoag's death had seemed genuine to him, as had his protestation of innocence with regards the fire. But now, hearing the order from his boss and conscious of the fact that the rest of the crew were waiting for him to cast his rope over Walt, he began to swing it.

Walt stepped back, pulled his horse's head around so that its neck provided a kind of battlement that made it impossible for Biff to get a rope over him. 'No one's putting a rope over me,' he told Ben Hoag. 'If there was a fire at your ranch, it had nothing to do with me. Nor did the death of your daughter.'

Using his knees, Biff Clayton guided his cow-pony towards the edge of the semi-circle, trying to find a position from which he could get a clear throw with his rope.

'I'm not going to let you do it, Biff,' warned Walt. His right hand reached for the butt of his holstered handgun.

'He's going for his gun,' someone yelled.

Walt drew and fired, the bullet smacked

into Biff Clayton's right shoulder, twisting him in the saddle and forcing him to drop the spinning rope.

Other riders reached for their guns, but Ben Hoag's voice barked at them before any shots were fired. 'Don't shoot him. That would be too easy for him. I want him to hang, to know some of the suffering he inflicted on my girl.'

In order to shoot Biff Clayton, it had been necessary for Walt to move away from the white stallion and, as a result of the gunshot, that horse had taken a couple of sideways steps that left Walt exposed to his adversaries. Finding cover became his priority. At first, he backed away then, espying a couple of cottonwoods a dozen yards to his left, he made a dash to reach them. The sound of running horses reached him and he threw a look over his shoulder as he ran. Another rider was approaching, the loop of his rope circling above his head. Without pausing, Walt swung his arm back and fired another shot. Harvey Jacks yelled as the bullet tore into his guts. He slumped forward then tipped off the side of his horse to lie writhing in the long grass.

The horse didn't slacken pace. For a moment, an opportunity seemed to offer itself to Walt. If he could mount the horse, there was the possibility of escape but no sooner had the thought occurred to him than it was dashed by his own negligence. He didn't see the hump of cottonwood root that had burst through the surface of the ground and he tumbled full length as the horse raced by. Adding to the disaster, his pistol fell from his hand and was lost from sight among the prairie grass.

Instantly, men were upon him, kneeling on his back to put an end to his struggles then tying his hands together to make resistance impossible.

Ben Hoag inspected the tree under which Walt had fallen. 'Bring his horse here,' he ordered Omaha, then told Chet Taylor to throw his rope over a low branch.

The sight of the noose renewed Walt's

fighting spirit but there was little he could do to prevent being lifted onto the back of his white stallion and the rope fixed around his neck.

'Whatever plans your father had to steal my land end here,' Ben Hoag told him but, like everything that had happened in the last few minutes, those words had no meaning for Walt.

A shout went up which brought a pause to the hurried proceedings. 'It's Frank,' Omaha informed the group and activity ceased until Ben's youngest son joined them.

The colour drained from Frank's face when he took in the situation. Not only was Walt Risby under the threat of death, but two of their own men were nursing gunshot wounds. Harvey Jacks was propped against the same tree that was to be Walt Risby's gallows, and the greyness of his face suggested that his life was not likely to extend much beyond the condemned man's.

'You mustn't do this,' Frank told his father. 'Take him to Marshal Tasker in

Stanton. Let him stand trial.'

'Tasker is in the pay of his father. There would never be a trial.'

'I'm innocent,' Walt Risby shouted, his voice tremulous, affected by the knowledge that Ben Hoag was convinced of his guilt and had no intention of removing the noose from his neck.

'I'm not certain it was Walt,' Frank said.

'Don't shame me,' said Ben. 'One rancher in this valley with a weak son is enough.' He turned his horse, rode alongside the condemned man and without another word, slapped the rump of the white stallion. It sprang forward, hobbled for a step or two then stood still.

Ben watched Walt Risby's throes until they ceased then, wordlessly, he led his men away from the hanging tree, leaving the body to sway gently in the breeze and the white stallion to peacefully graze.

8

Before riding away from the Diamond-H that morning, Silas Tasker promised Ben Hoag that he would question Walt Risby when he returned home, and that his neighbour's son would be put before a judge if there was any case to answer. But the marshal knew that even if he'd heard the words, they were insufficient to appease Ben Hoag. The boss of the Diamond-H hadn't budged an inch from his opinion that Walt was responsible for Mary's death, nor that he deemed it a crime for which the death penalty was the only suitable punishment. Moreover, Ben's need for revenge had been heightened by the events in Stanton the previous night, making the prospect of a war between the two largest ranches in the territory a matter of immediate concern.

When he returned to Stanton, Silas's first stop was at the telegraph office.

Although Jethro Humbo was able to assure Silas that there had been no hitch in sending the message to Miles City, there had as yet, been no response from Sheriff Brown. The marshal wasn't the only person disappointed by an inactive telegraph line; Mort Risby was hanging around town awaiting an answer from his son. The post office clerk confided to the lawman that Mort had been in his office several times that morning, anxious for a reply to the message he had sent. Although Jethro promised both men that he would deliver their messages the moment he received them, their visits to his office persisted throughout the day.

Silas Tasker had been surprised to find Mort Risby still in town when he returned from the Diamond-H, but the rancher's presence provided a small crumb of comfort; there would be no furtherance of hostilities between the two factions while Mort was twiddling his thumbs in Stanton. During that day, in fact, Mort was almost as regular a visitor at the marshal's office as he was at Jethro Humbo's. The main purpose of his visits was to niggle at Silas for the release of his imprisoned ranch-hands, but the town marshal was adamant that they would remain in his cells until their trial for murder. The rancher's attempts to obtain the release of Steve Tumbrell and Luke Bywater troubled Silas. The pair had shown an aptitude for violence and gunplay and the lawman wondered if it was those skills that Mort Risby wanted back on his payroll.

Mort Risby was annoyed by the marshal's refusal to release his men but he was even more angered by the lawman's pronouncement that Walt, too, would be arraigned before the judge if he couldn't prove he was in Miles City when the Diamond-H stable was set alight. Mort accused Silas of siding with the Hoags, insisted that his son was innocent and vowed he would never be charged with the crime.

In the late afternoon, Silas Tasker stepped outside and cast a look up the street, wondering if there was any value in another trip to the telegraph office, before crossing to the coffee house which was his usual practice at this hour. Further down the street he could see the men from the Triple-R who had loitered on the street with their boss all day. Lloyd Rafton and Davy Walsh were leaning against the wall of the River Bend Saloon while another two, Chuck Grainger and Benny Gates, lounged, almost sleepily, on seats that were set deep in the shadows of its long, sloped roof. Mort alone, seemed alert. He sat with his hands on his knees, displaying a rigidity to his body that epitomised his unyielding character.

From the opposite direction, the light jingle of harness drew Silas's attention. A one-horse buggy appeared in the distance and trudged slowly along the rutted main street. Silas watched its approach, gripped by a sense of foreboding. He recognized Abe Brewster's vehicle and stepped to the edge of the boardwalk to await his arrival.

The doctor drew his buggy alongside the marshal's office. His arrival had attracted the attention of other people, and from across the street there were signs of hurried activity. Men came running and troubled voices were raised, their interest awoken by the hobbling white horse that was tied to the back of the doctor's buggy.

'What's the trouble, Abe?' asked Silas Tasker.

The doctor turned and indicated the covered form in the space behind him. 'It's Walt Risby.'

Silas stepped onto the street and reached inside the buggy to uncover the dead man's face. 'Where did you find him?'

Before Abe Brewster answered, the men from across the street had surrounded the vehicle and Mort Risby, too, gazed on the face of his dead son.

'He was out on the range,' Abe Brewster announced, 'five or six miles from the river.'

'Who did it?' Mort Risby wanted to

know, but the glare he threw at Silas Tasker told the lawman that the rancher had already come up with his own answer.

Murmuring among the crowd increased as the identity of the victim was passed around, but most people remained silent, awaiting the reactions of the marshal and Mort Risby. The subdued atmosphere only lasted until a close bystander looked at the body and immediately understood the cause of the red burn mark around Walt's neck.

'They hanged him,' he shouted, 'the Hoags have hanged Walt Risby.'

Knowledge of Ben Hoag's threats was widespread though few had expected him to carry them out. He had a reputation for being morose but not for being violent. Like most people in the area he was regarded as a hardworking family man. But now, voices began to rise against him, reflecting the communal outrage at such an act. Silas yelled for order and when his voice wasn't loud enough to be heard over the uproar he drew his pistol and fired two shots into the air.

'Abe, I'll speak to you in my office.' He spotted the undertaker among the men standing along the boardwalk. 'Noah,' he said to him, 'take the doctor's buggy down to your workshop. The rest of you go about your business.' He had to issue that final order a second time before the crowd began to disperse and only then because Noah Pink took hold of the horse's bridle to lead it down the street with the corpse-carrying buggy in its wake.

Ashen-faced, Mort Risby sat on a seat beside the marshal's desk and listened to Abe Brewster's account of a visit to the Diamond-H which had led to the discovery of his son's body hanging from a cottonwood tree on the open range.

'Don Glasco came for me a short time after midday,' the doctor began. 'Told me there'd been some shooting and I was needed out at the Hoag place. Biff Clayton had a bullet in his shoulder and Harvey Jacks had one in his belly. I was able to patch up Biff but Harvey Jacks was dead before I got there. I thought they'd shot each other but that turned out not to be the case. Your son shot both of them.'

'Says who?' Mort Risby wanted to know.

'Ben Hoag and his son. Biff Clayton, Pete Simms and others.'

'And you believe them?'

'What I believe doesn't matter. What I know is that Harvey Jacks is dead, that there was an ugly lump of lead in Biff's shoulder and everyone I spoke to agreed that Walt fired those slugs with the intention of inflicting damage.'

'Why did he do it?' Mort wanted to know, his tone reflecting a belief that his son must have been provoked.

'According to Ben, Walt began shooting when they questioned him about the fire. He figured his reaction was an admission of guilt.'

'So, they hanged him.'

The room remained silent for several moments before Mort spoke again.

'What are you going to do about this,

marshal?'

'I'll talk to Ben Hoag.'

'Talk!'

'You know I have no jurisdiction for anything that happens on the open range, but I don't intend letting this explode into a range war.'

Mort Risby snorted with derision, the message clear enough that it was already too late for that. 'Ben Hoag's been seeking a fight,' he said, 'and now he has one.'

'Hold on there, Mort,' said Silas Tasker, 'don't go bringing your troubles into this town. I'll have no gunplay in Stanton and I'll ban you and your men at the first hint of a fight.'

'How do you intend to enforce that, marshal? You haven't got one deputy to support you.'

Silas knew that that was true, but he wasn't prepared to be cowed by the rancher. 'Go home, Mort. Cool off. Let the law sort out the trouble.'

They were brave words, but he had failed to prevent Ben Hoag carrying out his threat and he had little reason to believe he would be more successful with Mort Risby. He studied the rancher's face and could see the same dreadful sense of loss in those dull eyes that he had seen in Ben Hoag's earlier that day. Any words that might alleviate the oncoming struggle were not within his grasp. Fleeting thoughts that the families were even, that both had suffered loss, that an eye had been paid for with another eye, would never be acknowledged. For each, the death of a child was unjustified and retaliation was not only necessary to salve the pain but also inherent in each man's character. Mort Risby quit the marshal's office without another word.

'What'll you do now, Silas?' asked Abe Brewster.

'Pray, Abe. Pray that Sheriff Brown's response doesn't provide Walt Risby with an alibi for the night of the fire. That might be the only thing that prevents this town going up like a keg of gunpowder.'

Doctor Brewster went off to collect his rig from Noah Pink, leaving Silas with the observation, 'Looks like you've got trouble and I'm going to be very busy.'

★ ★ ★

Silas Tasker hadn't been the only person to ride away from the Diamond-H that morning with a troubled mind. Shortly after the marshal's departure, Tom Hoag had quit his home, burdened by his father's intransigence. He had seen the faces of the men in the yard who had witnessed the angry words thrown across the fence at the lawman and understood their stoic loyalty. They were aware of the circumstances that had given rise to the abrasive behaviour of their boss and understood the consequences that could arise from it. Some of them wouldn't want to be involved in a feud that would involve gunplay, but none of them would show that. They were paid to defend the Diamond-H, its property, livestock and crew, and no one would show reluctance to earn his money at the first intimation of a fight. Yet more than one pair of eyes had strayed in Tom's direction as though he had the ability to placate his father and resolve the matter peacefully.

But Tom had made one unsuccessful attempt that morning to reason with his father and, at that moment, was unable to summon up further arguments that might placate the elder Hoag. Over and over he'd repeated that Frank had not positively identified Walt as the man he'd seen riding away from the ranch, but Ben had responded to that with a dismissive grunt and walked away. Frank's input to the discussion had been negligible and had given Tom neither support nor encouragement to do combat with their father's opinion. Tom was frustrated by his brother's attitude, greater resolve was needed if a clash with the Triple-R was to be avoided, but Frank was like a man swept along in a current that he knew he was too weak to combat.

So Tom had thrown a saddle on his horse and ridden off to the northern range where he'd sent a fence-mending gang. Physical work, he hoped, would sweat away those mental impediments that were making it difficult to form a strategy. Clear thinking was needed if he was to succeed in dissuading his father from his entrenched attitude. He understood his father's desire for revenge, he too grieved for his sister, but he didn't agree that stepping beyond the law was the way to achieve it. The Diamond-H wouldn't prosper by it, nor would Mary have condoned it. Perhaps convincing his father of the latter was the key to persuading him to abandon his quest for revenge.

He stayed with the fence gang throughout the afternoon, but the hours of labour failed to shake off those thoughts by which he was plagued. His gloomy mood was transmitted to the hired-hands and they worked in awkward silence until the job was done. Tom parted from them when the wagon was loaded for the return journey to the ranchhouse. He'd decided to ride into Stanton and consult Doctor Brewster. He had no reason to suppose the medic could help him, indeed, he was sure that no medicine existed that could be prescribed to cure his father's condition, but he knew no one else who might have advice to offer.

Stanton was situated in the higher ground, above the grazing land, where there was water and lumber to satisfy the needs of the townspeople. Tom was following one of the many game trails that abounded among the wooded slopes, routes that were too narrow, steep or hazardous for wagon roads, but which provided a shorter and quicker route for those who were not strangers to the territory. His horse needed no guidance but carefully picked its way around trees and bushes as it continued uphill. They had crossed the road that had been established between Stanton and the river crossing and were still climbing when a movement above caught Tom's attention. It was a flash of light, the sun reflecting off something metal, polished bright. He stopped and looked uphill.

Briefly, Tom caught sight of a horseman but the mass of trees between them quickly hid him from view again. He remained still, watching for the rider to re-emerge at some visible point. Tom had no logical explanation for pausing, whoever the rider was, he would not belong to the crew of the Diamond-H. The higher trails wound away to the east, towards the headquarters of the Triple-R. Tom waited. He had no reason to avoid meeting a rider from the other ranch but in the circumstances, didn't want to risk aggravating an awkward situation. His eyes scanned the higher ground, eager to catch a glimpse of the rider who was heading away from the town which was Tom's destination. When he was sure their paths would not cross he would proceed.

When Tom next espied the horseman, he was almost directly above him, and he had company. There were another three men and Tom was able to put a name to two of them. Chuck Grainger was the ranch foreman and Davy Walsh had been on the Triple-R payroll for several years. Tom figured he probably knew the other two riders, but the heavily-wooded hillside was a hindrance to a clear view. Even so, he was aware that the four above had also reined their animals to a halt and had him under observation. He raised a hand, the standard greeting when cowboys met on the open range. Any act of normality, Tom told himself, would surely help to maintain peaceful relations between the two ranches.

The men of the Triple-R, however, had just left their boss attending to the details of his son's funeral. He'd ordered them back to the ranch with words that left little doubt in their minds that the Triple-R was at war with the Diamond-H. Despite the words of warning that had been issued by the town marshal, their commander-in-chief was Mort Risby and he demanded revenge for the death of his son. Furthermore, Walt had not only been the boss' son, he had been their friend, too. Davy Walsh raised his rifle and fired a shot at Tom Hoag. The bullet glanced off a tough spruce and sang its way down the hillside.

A second bullet zinged past Tom's

head and his yell of startled surprise brought a reaction from his horse. It skipped forward intending to continue along the game trail it had been following, but Tom whipped its head around and urged it downhill with shouts and kicks. Every step provided extra cover as the horse twisted between trees as rapidly as the terrain permitted. More shots sounded from the hillside above, but no slugs found a way through the woods to trouble Tom. Still, the yells of the riders warned him that they were in deadly pursuit.

Of necessity, each Triple-R rider was picking his own way down the hillside which effectively eliminated the possibility that Tom would be caught in a fusillade; when one man had an uninterrupted view of their fleeing quarry, the multitude of trees made it unlikely that a clear shot was available to another. Shots, however, were fired intermittently but with such haste that they were ineffective. Even so, Tom heard them strike trees, snap twigs and branches and was forced to keep as low as possible in the saddle while he attempted to escape.

Fighting back was out of the question. As yet, he hadn't even drawn his gun because he needed to keep his concentration on the route ahead. It was imperative to avoid the obstacles inherent with the trail he was following. He dipped under a low bough, swerved around a flowering chokecherry bush and emerged on the established trail. Deprived of the protection of the trees he had a decision to make. If he remained on the road he could demand a greater pace from his horse and perhaps, before they reached the road, would be able to put enough distance between himself and the Triple-R men that would put an end to their pursuit. He didn't know the reason for the attack but he was sure they wouldn't try to continue it in Stanton.

Suddenly, the calls of his hunters sounded too close to remain on the open road. He directed his horse among the trees of the slope that led back down to the grassland. That was the swiftest route back to Diamond-H land but there were miles of open terrain to cross before he reached it. His horse had travelled far since leaving the ranch that morning which made him unsure of its stamina if he had to outrun the work horses of the men behind him. He chose to avoid the game trail he'd used on his way up the hillside, hoping it would make his route more difficult to follow. It was still necessary to negotiate the close-growing trees but he tried to maintain a diagonal line of descent which would prolong his time among them. It was a gamble, a hope that he would be able to increase the gap between himself and his pursuers before he reached the grassland. Once there, he would need every advantage he could muster to reach his home without falling into their hands.

Disaster struck long before he reached the bottom of the hillside.

A leaf-covered root foxed the horse and it fell heavily, slithering down the soft slope, leaving Tom some distance behind. It shrieked with fright but although it collided with more than one tree in its path it escaped without any serious injury. When, eventually, it gained its feet, it continued apace downhill without a moment's thought for its dislodged rider.

Tom wasn't sure how he'd escaped injury but he'd managed to get his left leg out of the stirrup and across the horse's back before it became crushed under the animal. He knew the animal's cry would have pinpointed his location for the Triple-R men and even though they had not yet reached this part of the descent, the sound would spur their determination to capture him. When he saw his horse hurrying downhill without him he made no effort to catch it. Instead, he made use of some high-growing ferns at the base of an elm, lying flat among them, hoping the riders would be too intent upon their pursuit to notice him.

The ruse worked. Tom watched as one by one all four of his hunters passed the place where he lay. When they were out of sight he began the short climb back to the road. He had no alternative but to try to reach Stanton without being overtaken by the men from the Triple-R. He would talk with Silas Tasker; perhaps the marshal would be able to explain the action of Mort Risby's men.

A gunshot rang out from below and Tom guessed that one of the Triple-R men was shooting at shadows, but it caused him to quicken his pace. Distant voices drifted up to him and he wondered if they'd found the riderless horse. He hurried on and stumbled onto the road just as a two-horse buckboard hove into view. From behind came sounds of the Triple-R men riding back up the hillside. He hurried forward towards the buckboard which was already pulling to a halt. As he closed in on it the only thought in his head was that it might provide sanctuary, but in an instant, it was wiped from his mind. He recognized the driver and involving Clara Buxton in his troubles was the last thing he wanted to do.

'Who was shooting?' Clara asked.

Tom threw a glance behind, he knew it wouldn't be long before the Triple-R men, too, were on the road. 'They mean to kill me,' he told her because nothing else was relevant.

'Who?' she asked, but didn't wait for an answer. 'Hide,' she told him.

Tom aimed for the foliage at the other side of the road, but Clara, sitting high on the wagon box, could see the horsemen as they reached the far edge of the lower slope. 'Quickly,' she told him.

Bending low, Tom used the horses and wagon to hide him from sight. At the last moment, instead of taking refuge among the surrounding trees and flora, Tom slipped under the wagon. Grabbing the struts that held the axle bar of the rear wheel he hauled himself off the ground and rested his feet on the front axle bar. Silently he hung there, his arms beginning to ache before the horsemen reached the wagon.

It was Clara who spoke first, enquiring again about the shots she'd heard.

He recognized the voice of the second

speaker. Chuck Grainger didn't answer Clara's question but asked one of his own.

'Have you seen anybody along the road?'

'No. There was some movement back there. Higher up the hillside. I think it was just a deer.'

Tom could see the feet of the horses, knew the men had stopped abreast of the wagon.

'You'd best get home, Miss Buxton,' another voice advised. 'Get home and stay there for a few days.'

'Why?'

'There's going to be trouble. Big trouble.'

'What's happened, Benny?'

'Walt Risby's been killed. The Hoags lynched him.'

9

Clara Buxton was motionless as the men rode away in search of their fugitive, resuming their hunt in the false location she'd indicated. Slowly they climbed the slope, wending their way between trees until they were lost from sight. Clara was transfixed by the news imparted by Benny Gates, wondering how the friendliness she was accustomed to could have descended so quickly into turmoil. Two days ago, she'd had a best friend who'd shared her hopes and her pleasures but since Mary's death nothing had been the same. Misery and trouble had replaced the smiles and happy greetings that had been the normal characteristics of the local people.

It had begun with the hurried, almost indecent funeral that had taken place at the Diamond-H. Ben Hoag's heartache at the loss of his daughter was understandable, as was his desire to have her buried alongside her mother, but, in Clara's opinion, Mary had deserved greater respect than to be put in the ground without a gathering of friends to say their last goodbyes. Not even a coffin had been constructed for her, buried in canvas like a pioneer crossing the plains. That might have been acceptable for her mother seven years earlier when there were barely enough properties to call the settlement a town, but now there were civic buildings denoting the progress of the living and a consecrated cemetery for the dead.

Yet despite her overall dissatisfaction with the funeral and the brusque treatment that she and Mrs Brewster had received from Ben Hoag, it was the hostile reception afforded to Mort Risby that remained the most unpleasant memory of that day. Each time she recalled that confrontation she was chilled by its attendant threat of violence. She remembered the glances of murderous anger that had flashed between the two men and the correspondingly uneasy stances that had been adopted by those at their backs. That atmosphere of impending fury had hung around the Hoags' yard even after the departure of the men from the Triple-R and, she had learned during her recent visit to Stanton, become manifest with the killing of Buck Downs.

The gunfight in the River Bend had been the prime topic of conversation in the general store where Clara had been delivering fruit and eggs. Her family had begun supplying such produce during Gus Hubber's ownership and had continued to do so with the arrival of the Danvers. Although Clara had not joined Cora Hope's gossip circle in the front part of the premises, their raised exclamations of outrage still reached her as she stacked the baskets she had brought behind the rear counter. It was Joe Danvers who filled in the details for her as they worked.

She was chilled by the knowledge that the fight had involved men from the Triple-R and Diamond-H ranches but surprised by the reaction of Joe Danvers. If she entertained thoughts that the shooting of Buck Downs was a precursor to more violence, the store-owner seemed inclined to regard the incident as one typical of an isolated range town. Indeed, Clara had the impression that he was enjoying some reflected glory in his own part of the fist fight that had followed the gunplay.

Clara estimated Joe's age in the late-thirties and had always considered him to be a timid man; polite, helpful, smart in appearance and intelligent, but timid. He was talkative, seemingly interested in the well-being of every customer and their family, a useful talent, Clara supposed, for someone who dealt with the public every day. His wife, four or five years younger, was more reserved. Not unwilling to be sociable but reluctant to listen to or repeat tittle-tattle. Joe was dominant in the store, but Clara suspected that the more thoughtful Beth Danvers was the prominent partner in their marriage.

That opinion, however, was dented as

the last of the fruit was unloaded from the buckboard and brought indoors. The attention of one of the gossips had been attracted to some event further down the street. People were congregating outside the marshal's office.

'It looks like Doctor Brewster's buggy,' the woman declared. The prospect of fresh information over which they could gossip was strong enough to lure them from the store and go hurrying down the street.

'I wonder what's happened,' Joe said, rubbing his hands on his apron and making his way towards the door.

'Don't go,' Beth said.

'I'll only be a few minutes,' he told her. 'It looks like something important.'

'Please, Joe,' she implored.

Joe Danvers looked around the store. Apart from Clara, only one other customer remained in the shop. 'Everyone will want to know what's happening down the street,' he told her. 'I'll be back before we fill up with customers again.' Then he was gone, hurrying past the window, eager to know the cause of the growing throng.

Clara had gathered up some empty baskets and taken them out to the wagon for the trip home, but there were purchases to make so she re-entered the store through the alley door she'd been using to unload her goods. In the middle of store, Jack Temple, the barber who had been the remaining customer when Joe Danvers had quit the building, was standing close to Beth, creating a tableau that perturbed Clara. Jack Temple loomed over the storekeeper's wife, his dark features heavy with menace, his lips stretched in a lupine-like grimace. Beth Danvers, head bowed, seemed to be in the process of drawing away from him but was somehow prevented from doing so.

Abruptly, Clara stopped, taking in the scene before her. Jack Temple raised his eyes so that his gaze met Clara's over Beth's shoulder. He muttered something which Clara was unable to hear but which drew the colour from the other young woman's face, then turned on his heel and left the store.

When Beth turned to face Clara, an unconvincing smile touched her face. She stepped around her to go behind a counter.

'Beth!' Clara's utterance was both an enquiry in connection with the other's welfare and an opportunity for her to give an explanation for what had taken place. When she didn't get an immediate answer she asked, 'Was he threatening you?'

'What makes you think that?' Beth Danvers tried to laugh to dissuade Clara from such a line of questioning. 'Of course not, he was just checking up on stock he'd ordered.'

Clara didn't believe her and red marks around Beth's wrists showed that Jack Temple had been gripping them tightly to prevent her from escaping his attentions. She remembered how Beth had tried to prevent her husband leaving and figured it was because she was afraid to be alone with Jack Temple. She wanted to pursue the matter, insist that Beth inform her husband about the barber's behaviour, but she wasn't a confidante of the storekeeper's wife, therefore reluctant to interfere. By the time she'd filled her shopping order, however, she could see movement on the street again. Whatever cause people had had to assemble at the marshal's office had been resolved and Joe Danvers would soon be returning to the store.

As she drove out of town, Clara hoped that Beth would tell her husband the truth about Jack Temple's visit, but wasn't certain that she would. It was another troubling episode, another shadow over Stanton that seemed laden with trouble.

Then had come the gunshots, followed by the words of Benny Gates which echoed and re-echoed in her head. The Hoags have lynched Walt Risby. Two days ago, she would have denied the possibility of that family taking the law into its own hands but now she had to give the matter serious thought. What she knew of the Hoags had been garnered from her friendship with Mary. The warmth that the dead girl had held for her father and brothers had induced her own affection for them, most acutely for Tom in whom she had begun to harbour hopes for a future together. She was attracted to him by the quiet, resolute manner in which he conducted the business of the ranch, seeing in him a man capable of providing a secure and happy life. But how much did she really know about the man who, even now, was hiding under her wagon, a refugee from an atrocious deed, a fugitive condemned to be shot on sight by his neighbours. Wordlessly, she waited, her mind troubled by the possibility that harbouring Tom Hoag was a mistake.

When he emerged, however, it took only the briefest glance at his face for Clara to know that the announcement of Walt Risby's killing had been no less a surprise to him than it had been to her. For a moment, his eyes were turned towards the hillside, seeking out the Triple-R riders who could still be heard as they continued their hunt for him.

'I need to find my horse,' he muttered. 'I'll speak to Silas Tasker.'

She remembered the activity outside the marshal's office that had drawn Joe Danvers away from his store. It seemed probable that that incident was connected to the death of Walt Risby. 'You can't go into town,' she said. 'I saw Mort Risby there. There might be other Triple-R riders with him.'

'I've got to know the truth,' Tom told her.

'Come back to the farm with me,' she suggested. 'You can use one of our horses to get back to the Diamond-H.'

Tom refused to be deterred. If something had happened to Walt Risby, he needed to know what evidence existed of his family's culpability. He thanked Clara for coming to his rescue but insisted upon setting off downhill to find his missing animal.

'Tom,' she called, her voice momentarily stopping his descent, 'be careful.'

Tom acknowledged the words with a

curt nod but the dreadful possibility that his father had carried out his threats so occupied his mind that Clara's words were forgotten as soon as he took another step. Anxious to be re-united with his horse, he slithered through the shale and loose topsoil as he went rapidly down the slope. The sound of Clara's departing buckboard reached him but the density of the forest soon distorted the direction from which it came. It wasn't a conscious thought but primeval instinct which reminded him that he needed still to be wary of his pursuers. Currently, they were chasing shadows, but they might resume their search for him in this part of the wood at any moment. All that was required was for someone to put two and two together and arrive at the conclusion that he might have need of his horse. So he moved as quickly as the terrain permitted and listened for the jingle of harness, the scuffing of hoofs on the ground or voices bouncing off trees, the telltale signs that his hunters were close behind.

In fact, when he came face-to-face with Benny Gates, it was a completely unexpected encounter for both men. Tom hadn't given any consideration to the possibility that any of the Triple-R riders could already be lower down the hillside but, because Clara Buxton's information had not been totally conclusive and he didn't want Tom Hoag to escape their clutches, Chuck Grainger had ordered Benny to patrol the lower slopes while the rest of the band took to the higher ground.

At first, when Tom stepped around the wide trunk of the pine he thought he'd found his own horse, but he was confused by the fact that someone was astride its back. The animal was standing still but it turned its head to look at Tom when he stepped into view. The blaze on its face revealed the error of his thinking. It took a moment for him to react, to try to dodge back behind the tree out of Benny's immediate view.

Benny's attention was fixed on something off to his right and it was only the shuffling of his mount, coupled with Tom's abrupt dash for cover that altered the focus of his attention.

'Hey!' he shouted and at the same moment raised his right arm.

Tom looked over his shoulder and could see a pistol in Benny's hand. Tom wasn't a gunfighter but even if he'd been as good as John Wesley Hardin, he doubted his ability to win a duel under the current circumstances. What saved him from death, however, was the fact that Benny Gates wasn't a killer either. Tom could see the eyes of the other man widen as he considered what was expected of him.

'Hey!' Benny called again, his voice relaying his reluctance to shoot to kill. Nonetheless, he pulled the trigger, the bullet exploding from the barrel into the sky above.

Tom was running now, putting in use the same tactics he'd used earlier when mounted, dodging between trees and around bushes to prevent Benny Gates from getting a clear shot at him. From behind came the report of another gunshot and again he suspected that it had been fired into the air but he couldn't be sure that Benny's mercy would continue. If Benny didn't shoot Tom he would have to explain his failure to those members of the Triple-R crew who would have less scruples in the matter. Tom figured that the prospect of their scorn was running through Benny's brain at that moment. The more times Benny pulled the trigger the greater grew the possibility that he'd succumb to their arguments and judge it his duty to put a bullet in Tom. Even if he didn't, the gunshots must have carried to the other riders who would, by now, be racing back down the hillside to assist in his capture.

For the moment, Tom's only plan was to evade Benny Gates. Behind him he could hear sounds of pursuit but couldn't risk looking back because he needed to watch every stride, every footfall, to avoid tripping or colliding with an obstacle that would knock him off his feet. On foot, he had greater manoeuvrability and was able to wend his way among the trees with greater alacrity than the sure-footed cow pony that Benny sat astride, but at the bottom of the wooded slope, when he reached the pasture land, he would be overtaken in moments. Even hopes of finding his own horse offered little comfort, knowing that soon, Benny Gates wouldn't be the only man behind him carrying a gun.

A bullet ricocheted off a nearby tree, spurring Tom to greater effort. A lump of bark had been torn away at head height; Benny was losing the fight with his conscience, had lowered his aim in order to put an end to the chase. Tom knew that any success on Benny's part meant his own death. Even a wound would slow him down sufficiently to give the rest of the Triple-R riders time to catch up.

Another shot was fired. Tom weaved away to his left, slithering a little way down the slope, trying desperately to maintain his balance as he avoided a large pine only to stumble into a thick chokecherry bush. He hoped that Benny was armed with only one gun. He hadn't counted the bullets that had been fired but figured that Benny couldn't have more than one live shell in his gun. The dual task of keeping an eye on his quarry and keeping his horse on a secure route of pursuit would have deprived him of the opportunity to reload.

Fleetingly, the notion to make a stand passed through Tom's mind. No blame could be attached if he chose to defend himself, if he sheltered behind the next wide tree and shot Benny Gates.

Standing still, his aim would be surer than that of the on-coming horseman. He had never shot a man before, but he'd hit snakes and wolves and Benny was much bigger than those creatures. But even though his own life was under threat, he realized a reluctance to shoot at the Triple-R man.

The decision, however, was taken out of his hands when his foot became entangled in the clinging chokecherry fronds. He went down, sprawling and rolling down the leaf-strewn slope. Tom gave no voice to the pain occasioned to his left shoulder by the awkward landing, and paid little heed to the minor cuts and grazes he received. His immediate concern was the proximity of his hunter, wondering if he was already under his gun and would be despatched without any opportunity to declare himself innocent of Walt Risby's death; shot down like a rabid dog.

Scrambling to his knees Tom looked around. At first, he couldn't see Benny Gates but close at hand he could hear movement. It wasn't the rapid approach of a hunter anxious to be in at the kill. When Tom espied his pursuer, he realized that his tumble had been unobserved. Benny was moving cautiously, scanning the woods, trying to catch sight of his prey in order to continue the hunt. Drifting from further up the hillside came the first sounds of other activity, the rest of the Triple-R riders were drawing closer. Unseen, he watched Benny moving ever nearer and wondered if he would have to shoot him in order to escape. But gunfire was to be avoided. It would pinpoint his location to the riders above. It was at that moment that he realized his hand was resting on a long branch and a plan to utilize it sprang instantly to his mind. Rising carefully to his feet, he positioned himself behind a tree which Benny was due to pass.

The Triple-R man was taken completely by surprise when the thick bough came over his horse's head and crashed into his chest. With a yell his arms were flung wide and he was knocked to the ground. Winded, he was unable to resist Tom's continued attack. The pistol was kicked from his hand and a punch delivered to his jaw. Dazed, Benny watched as Tom Hoag picked up the fallen gun, fearing that he was about to be killed with his own weapon. Tom stood over him, anxiously looking uphill where the sounds of approaching riders were becoming louder.

'I had nothing to do with Walt Risby's death,' he said, then threw Benny's gun away, further down the slope.

Thoughts of finding his own horse had long since been driven from Tom's mind. Now, he gathered up the reins of Benny's work pony and climbed into the saddle. He set the animal at a downhill run, anxious to be free of the restrictive woodland. His destination remained the town of Stanton and he figured he could only get there by outrunning the band of men from the Triple-R. Heading for town across the grasslands was a longer route but there were no obstacles along the way to prevent a flat-out run. If he was far enough ahead when he reached the grasslands he was confident that he would not be overtaken during the three-mile run. The only cause for concern was the fact that he was riding another man's horse. He knew the capabilities of his own animal but was ignorant of the effort that had been asked of the one under him before he'd climbed into the saddle.

He was a furlong across the grassland before he heard the first cries of pursuit. A couple of wasted gunshots sounded in his wake. They were no threat to his life, but they served to concentrate his mind on the ride ahead. A glance over his shoulder revealed only two riders in pursuit. He wondered if the others meant to intercept him by using another route to town. That was a plan he deemed unlikely to succeed and spurred on the horse he was astride.

About a mile from town the horse began to sag. Its stride began to shorten as huge flecks of foam flew off its hide. Behind, the chasing men had halved the gap by which they were separated, and the crack of pistol shots again carried to him. Tom shouted in the horse's ear and flipped at its flanks with the leather rein. The appearance of the first buildings of Stanton boosted his belief that he would safely reach the town.

A bullet passed close to his head and another look back showed that the Triple-R riders had further reduced the gap; their horses were clearly running stronger than his own. More shots were fired, and he crouched low to provide

162

his pursuers with the smallest possible target. Their efforts to shoot him continued as he rode into Stanton, causing those who were on the street to scuttle to the safety of the buildings.

Only one man remained on the street. He stepped off the boardwalk as Tom hauled his weary pony to a halt outside the marshal's office. Silas Tasker raised his pistol and fired a shot in the air, a warning to the two men in Tom's wake that he wouldn't tolerate any more gunfire on the streets of his town.

Chuck Grainger, his smoking pistol still in his hand, yelled a warning at the marshal. 'He killed Walt and we mean to see that he pays for it.'

'You'll put your gun away and get off the street. If Tom Hoag is guilty of Walt Risby's death he'll face a judge like any other criminal.'

Marshal Tasker's words weren't enough to appease the angry Triple-R man. His intention to shoot again was clear to all those watching. Tom was only five yards away now, a sitting target for the armed man, but the shot he fired never found its mark. Silas Tasker was the first man to pull the trigger. His bullet struck the ground close to the front hoofs of Chuck Grainger's mount. The horse reared and as Chuck slid off over its tail he discharged his gun into the air. By the time he'd regained his feet, Silas had hustled Tom into his office and closed the door.

10

'Is it true,' Tom Hoag asked, facing Silas Tasker across the scarred, old desk at which the marshal conducted business, 'is Walt Risby dead?'

Silas eyed the rancher's son, tried to penetrate the younger man's show of confusion, tried to determine if he was as ignorant of the facts as his words and expression implied. Eventually, he responded with a brief but indisputable nod of assent.

Many questions flicked through Tom's mind; although it was difficult to pass off Walt's death and his father's threats as an unhappy coincidence, he still needed to know the surrounding circumstances that had led to the Triple-R riders adopting a shoot-on-sight philosophy.

It was Silas, however, who framed the first question, wanting an account of Tom's activities since they'd parted at the Diamond-H earlier that day. He jotted down the names of Casey Brogan and Johnny Wells, the two men that Tom had worked alongside in the north pasture. Then he told Tom what he knew of the events down by the Dearborn, but dwelt on the fact that although the killing of Harvey Jacks and the wounding of Biff Clayton were evidence that Walt Risby had been actively involved in the fight, they didn't provide irrefutable proof that he had been the instigator of the violence.

'It's hard to believe that any man would choose to launch a single-handed attack against seven. If he was guilty of burning down your out-building it seems more likely that he would avoid your father, not get close enough to engage in a pistol fight.'

'Seven.' Tom knew that some of their cattle were grazing on the open range towards the river but was at a loss to understand why so many men had been needed to tend to them.

Silas Tasker interrupted his thoughts. 'I can't ignore this, Tom. My responsibility is for the maintenance of law in Stanton and I'll do my best to make sure that any trouble between your family and Mort Risby is kept out of town. But no matter what efforts are made to keep feuds like this out on the range they eventually lead to more and more acts of violence with armies of gunmen brought in to propound the theory that might is right. When that happens, every citizen suffers. Neither your pa nor Mort Risby will allow me to investigate so I'll have to get a message to Helena to request aid from State officers.' He paused a moment to let the implication of his action sink in. To ensure his meaning was clear, he said, 'If laws have been broken, the guilty will be punished.'

Tom Hoag considered the marshal's words, analysed them and reached the conclusion that the lawman was as dissatisfied as himself with the explanation of Walt Risby's death. If, like Harvey Jacks and Biff Clayton, the young man had collected a bullet in a gunfight, the circumstances of his death might have been less suspicious, but to be hanged after the skirmish had a veneer of cold-bloodedness that didn't sit easy with either of them. Guided by family loyalty, he kept his thoughts to himself but, in any case, any continuation of their conversation was brought to an end by loud pounding on the barred office door.

After Chuck Grainger had been unhorsed, the men of the Triple-R had remained outside the marshal's office and were soon joined by other townsmen drawn to that end of town by the gunfire that had heralded the arrival of the cowboys. Benny Gates had gone looking for the boss of the Triple-R and found him in Noah Pink's Funeral Parlour making arrangements with its proprietor for the burial of his son. Now, Mort Risby was thumping on the marshal's door with his fist and yelling for admittance.

A glance through the small window revealed to Silas that more than a dozen men were assembled outside the office door and though the expressions on the faces of the townsmen showed little more than curiosity, those of the Triple-R riders were etched with determined anger.

'Come on, Marshal,' Mort Risby called, 'open up.'

Silas grabbed a shotgun from a wall-mounted gun rack. 'Step away from the door,' he shouted back. 'I'm not coming out until you've moved off the boardwalk onto the street.'

A further glimpse out of the window provided confirmation of what he expected; the townspeople had moved away from the door as ordered but the Triple-R men had merely taken a few steps to the side, remaining on the wooden walkway outside his office. Mort Risby had barely moved before renewing his demand for the door to be opened.

Silas motioned for Tom to open the door but told him to close and re-bar it as soon as he'd stepped outside. Tom obeyed.

With the shotgun grasped at both ends, Silas left his office. As expected, he was immediately confronted by the broad figure of Mort Risby. The marshal thrust his weapon roughly against the rancher's chest and pushed. The manoeuvre took Mort Risby completely by surprise, no one had manhandled him in such a manner for many years. He was an important man in these parts and such disrespect was totally unexpected. He stumbled, lost his footing at the edge of the planking and sprawled in the dusty street.

'I told you to step away from the door,' Silas growled at him, unrepentant for the rancher's embarrassment.

'We want that man in there.' Mort Risby, red-faced with anger, threw out the demand as he was being helped to his feet by two of his workers. 'He killed my son.'

'I have no evidence that Tom Hoag has killed anyone, so I suggest you all disperse and go about your business.'

No one moved, but Silas had never believed himself blessed with those oratory skills capable of swaying the opinion of a mob. The gesture he made with the shotgun, however, was more effective. One or two men began to move across the street while others shuffled their feet as though they would soon follow. He held eye contact with Mort Risby, knowing the rancher wouldn't easily back down, wouldn't wish to appear impotent in front of his men or the people of Stanton. 'Go home, Mort,' he said. 'There's nothing to be gained hanging around here.'

'It's Mr Risby to you, Tasker,' said the rancher, 'and I'll decide for myself when the time is right for me to leave town.'

'Let's come to an understanding,' the marshal told him, 'if anything happens to Tom Hoag, then you are the first man I'll be looking for.'

'Are you setting yourself up as his protector, marshal?'

'No. The law is his protector.'

'You only represent the law here in town,' Mort Risby reminded him.

'I'll tell you the same thing I told Tom Hoag. This feud has to end and I'm sending for State officers to intervene. So, don't consider setting an ambush for Tom Hoag when he leaves town because they'll search out wrongdoers and have the authority to punish them wherever their crimes are committed. Five years ago you got away without punishment when Sheriff Brown was summoned but you won't be so lucky another time.'

Mort Risby wasn't accustomed to being spoken to in such a threatening manner and he wasn't prepared to mildly quit the scene.

'You'll have to hope they respond to your telegraph message more quickly than the sheriff in Miles City. If you ever sent one.'

'I sent one.'

'Perhaps you've held onto the reply.'

'Why would I do that?'

'To protect your friends, the Hoags. My boy didn't start that fire and when his innocence is established you'll be forced to admit that they lynched him without reason. Perhaps you don't want to face up to the fact, but your friends murdered Walt.'

'The Hoags are my friends in exactly the same way I've always considered you to be. They aren't getting special treatment.'

'Prove it. If you haven't got Tom Hoag locked up then release my men, too.'

'Luke Bywater and Steve Tumbrell stay where they are until the judge hits town. I hope their crime is a separate issue because if I thought they'd killed Buck Downs at your bidding, you'd be in the vacant cell at the back of my office.'

Silas Tasker hefted his shotgun meaningfully which brought a scowl from Mort Risby before he turned his back on the marshal and crossed the street. Silas knocked on the door and told Tom Hoag it was safe to open up.

The stomach-churning apprehension that gripped Clara Buxton when she heard the renewal of gunfire took her by surprise. The crackles were neither close enough nor loud enough to earn such a reaction. She wasn't in danger from flying lead but instantly, she pulled the team to a halt, twisted on the seat and looked back along the trail. The place where she'd recently parted from Tom Hoag was no longer in view, obscured now by the wooded slope that the eastern route descended, but she continued to look in that direction as though the thought to return there was sitting firmly in her mind. There could be no doubt that the sounds she had heard had been gunshots and their message was clear enough; the Triple-R riders had found Tom. For several moments she was overwhelmed by a numbing emptiness. All sense of purpose and action deserted her. The sensation that the world she had known no longer existed became even more dizzying and frightening. The thought held her for only a moment, until it was broken by more reports of distant gunfire.

Mentally, she shook herself free of the constraining experience, forced herself to face the grim truth. Tom Hoag was in trouble. It was possible that he had been caught by his enemies, perhaps killed by them, and she felt impelled to act on his behalf. Common sense told her to head for home as quickly as possible. A feud between ranchers wasn't her concern and it probably only meant trouble for any outsider who interfered, but he was Mary's brother and for that reason alone he was deserving of her assistance.

Cracking the whip over the heads of the horses she set the team in motion again, slapping the reins and yelling at them until they were soon at full gallop along the trail. As she urged them onwards she confessed to herself that being her dead friend's brother wasn't her only reason for trying to help Tom Hoag. She was able to forgive the terse tone of their recent, brief meeting and the abrupt manner of his departure because they had been dictated by circumstances. What she recalled most vividly was the look of trust in his eyes when he'd stumbled onto the road in search of sanctuary from his pursuers. He had had no doubt at that moment that she would provide it.

She turned off the trail and headed south across the grasslands, racing the horses to their very limit, recklessly bouncing the wagon over ruts and raised clumps as they ate up the miles towards her new destination. Her parents would wonder at the reason for her late return home, but she would explain it all to them when she got there.

Two things surprised Clara when she reached the gate of the Diamond-H ranch-house; it was closed and guarded by two armed men.

'Tom's in trouble,' she told the man she knew only as Omaha when he asked her business. 'Triple-R men mean to kill him.'

The gate was opened, and she was taken to the house where Ben Hoag listened to her account of his son's plight.

'He was hoping to reach Stanton,' Clara concluded. 'He wanted to learn about Walt Risby's death from Marshal Tasker.'

She'd left the ranch after that, Matty Slade telling her to get home quickly because there would be bloodshed in Stanton if anything had happened to Tom.

News of Tom's misadventure soon

176

spread to the bunkhouse and every available man checked the shells in his pistol and rifle before heading to the corral to select a suitable mount for the ride into town. Six men were saddled up and ready to go when Ben Hoag left the house with his son, Frank, at his heels. Some of the men sensed tension between father and son but that wasn't unusual. Neither Hoag spoke, not to each other nor to the assembly of cowboys. Ben Hoag acknowledged their presence with a nod of his head then mounted up and led the men away from the ranch. A gap of ten lengths separated that group from Frank.

11

Trading had ended for the day in the mercantile store. In the lamplight, Joe Danvers was bent over a ledger, assessing his stock levels and calculating his takings. Beth Danvers finished tying the ribbons of her bonnet and picked up the basket that was waiting on the counter. Among the attributes that had cemented Beth's popularity in Stanton was her willingness to deliver orders to the homes of three infirm citizens. In normal circumstances, delivery boys were used for such errands but, for these three ageing and ailing women, it had become Beth's habit to provide a personal service. Her visits were a welcome break from their housebound tedium and she listened to their reminiscences as eagerly as they attended to her revelations of the latest local events.

Opening the street door, Beth walked out into the closing greyness of the day.

If the pair exchanged words it was done with the minimum of fuss; Beth appeared to be totally involved in arranging the heavy basket on her arm in order to twist the door fastener and Joe raised neither hand nor head in farewell, so engrossed was he in the figures on the page he was studying.

Outside, lamps burned at several points along Stanton's main street. Unusually, men loitered within those areas of yellowish glow, their presence on the street adding to the air of terrible expectancy that had swelled throughout the day, relegating earlier events to mere tasters of what was to come. Beth gripped her cloak as though warding off chill air, but the night was balmy, and her protective action was psychologically inspired rather than a measure to combat any physical discomfort. She had become enmeshed in a situation for which her only guilt was sympathy but if there was any truth in the rumours she'd overheard, it was possible that her silence had contributed to the dreadful lynching of Walt Risby.

She couldn't recall the circumstances that had first caused Frank Hoag to reveal his dissatisfaction with ranch life or his father's disinterest in his abilities, but she'd listened to him that day and on other occasions when he'd visited the general store. Of course, she knew she shouldn't have invited him into her home when Joe was in Miles City, even if it was only to share a cup of coffee, but he'd wanted her to know that he'd decided to quit the Diamond-H and planned to light out for California the next day.

Understandably, the death of his sister had put an end to that scheme, but the subsequent rumour linking Walt Risby to the fire at the Diamond-H had surprised her. After leaving her, there had only been sufficient time for Frank to get back to the ranch. He couldn't have followed anyone to the Dearborn and back. Perhaps he'd told that story to protect her reputation, but it would have been better that she suffered the scorn of Mrs Hope and her friends than that Walt Risby should be falsely tarred with the crime of murder. Now, Walt was dead, and in retaliation, an attempt had been made on the life of Tom Hoag. The whole town seemed to be holding its breath in anticipation of the next act, braced for an eruption of violence. The thought flashed through Beth's mind that perhaps a confession could prevent more bloodshed, that she should tell the truth to Marshal Tasker.

Unwillingly, Beth glanced at the barber shop across the street. It was in darkness, Jack Temple, too, had finished business for the day. She wondered if he was one of the figures she could see further down the street, exchanging thoughts and opinions with townsmen curious as to what the next outrage would be and where and when it would occur. A more troublesome possibility speared its way through her musing; perhaps he was standing in the dark depths of his barber shop, watching her even now as she paused on the sidewalk boards above the dry, hard-packed street.

A sudden movement to her right drew a gasp from her. A shape, a man pushed away from the wall against which he'd been leaning. He stepped forward, almost lurched and for a dreadful moment Beth believed it was Jack Temple. She took a pace backwards as though preparing to return to the security of the store.

'Didn't mean to startle you, Mrs Danvers.'

Beth didn't recognize the voice but noted a slight slur, suggesting it belonged to a man who had had more than his share of whiskey this day. 'Who is it?' she asked.

'Jimmy Carson, Mrs Danvers.'

'What are you doing here, Jimmy?' Beth didn't really care, she was just relieved that it wasn't Jack Temple waiting in the shadows for her.

'Don't rightly know,' the young timber-worker admitted. 'Guess I'm trying to hide.'

'Are you in trouble, Jimmy? Is someone chasing you?'

There was a self-deprecating lilt to the

brief chuckle that preceded Jimmy Carson's words. 'Reckon I'm trying to hide from myself,' he said. 'It's not easy to do.'

'I don't suppose it is,' she replied, thinking it was a trick she, too, would like to perfect.

'Some people are saying that Walt deserved to hang because he left me to walk home. Talking like I should be pleased he's dead. That was no reason for Walt to die. He wasn't bad. He was my friend. I just don't understand it, Mrs Danvers.'

'I'm sorry, Jimmy.' Beth knew her words were little comfort to the young man but there was little else she could say.

'People in the River Bend are talking about nothing else but Walt's lynching,' Jimmy told her. 'I don't want to listen.' He shook his head as though trying to loosen from his brain words and ideas that had no reason to be there. 'Just because I was left to walk home doesn't mean that Walt would set fire to Ben Hoag's barn. How can he think that?

Why didn't he ask my opinion? I would have told him the truth.'

'Of course you would, Jimmy.' Jimmy's implied counsel that all harm would be avoided by telling the truth chimed with Beth's own recent opinion. It was too late to help Walt Risby but it might prevent further violence. Frank Hoag had already decided to leave the territory and although he would now be banished with a blackened character, it was, in Beth's opinion, better than being the cause of further bloodshed. 'Joe is working on his books,' she said, indicating the interior of the store. 'Go in. You can hide there with a cup of coffee until you're ready to return to the River Bend.'

He grinned. 'I don't think I'll be going back there tonight. I'll just stay quiet out here for a while before I collect my horse and return home.'

'Goodnight then,' she said and stepped down on to the street.

'Mrs Danvers,' he called, he was looking down the street at the several points where men had gathered, 'be careful.

There's trouble brewing down the street.'

'Thank you, Jimmy, but I'm not going that way. I'm taking these groceries to Mrs Winterwhite.'

Beth crossed the street then cut down the first narrow alley which was the route to Mrs Winterwhite's small, isolated house on the rising ground that overlooked the livery stable and its corrals. Emerging from the alley, Beth was heading for the high timber structure that was Marley's stable when she heard the scuff of a hurried footfall behind her. For a moment, she assumed that the person trying to catch up was Jimmy Carson coming for the horse he'd presumably left in one of the corrals behind the stable. But she was wrong. Another three steps and she felt a hand grasp the upper part of her arm that carried the basket. She tried to shrug it off, but Jack Temple was not prepared to release her.

From the window of his unlit shop he'd watched as she'd left the general store and paused in conversation with Jimmy Carson. When she'd crossed the street he'd guessed her destination and slipped out the rear of his own premises to intercept her.

'Mrs Winterwhite can do without her provisions for a while longer,' he said. 'You're not putting me off any longer. No one will see us.' He tried to drag her back to the rear entrance of the barber shop and his upstairs living quarters.

'No,' she protested. 'I won't.'

'You know the alternative,' he hissed. 'Think about the effect it will have on your husband and your reputation in this community. You'll be ruined when I tell people what you've been up to.'

Again, Beth shook her head and tried to pull away, but Jack Temple tightened his grip until he was hurting her.

'Not just what you've been doing but who you've been doing it with and when,' he said. 'What do you think Marshal Tasker will do when he knows the truth? You'll probably wind up in the State prison.'

'Let go of me,' she said. She tried to push him away, needed to drop the basket because the pain in her arm was now intense.

Jack Temple yanked her in the direction he wanted her to go, seemed prepared to pull her all the way back to his shop, mouthing threats and insults as he did so. Incensed by her struggles he turned and raised his arm in readiness to deliver an open-handed slap to her face, but it was a blow that was never delivered. His wrist was caught by another's hand and he was pulled away from his victim.

With both hands and with greater strength than Jack Temple anticipated, Jimmy Carson pushed against the barber's chest. Caught by surprise, he stumbled as he was propelled backwards. Jimmy's words, an angry demand, barely registered with Jack Temple as he crashed against the thick corral rails. 'What are you doing to Mrs Danvers?'

'Keep out of it,' replied Jack Temple. 'This is between me and her.'

Beth had moved away to stand against the back wall of one of the main street properties. The look he threw at her seemed to bear the expectation of corroboration.

When none came, young Jimmy Carson stepped between them, confronting Jack Temple and defending Beth Danvers. His hands curled into fists, stressing the point that Jack Temple faced a fight if he didn't immediately quit the scene.

Jack was more heavily built than Jimmy, looked capable of dishing out a beating to the younger man and with a powerful swing of his right arm, attempted to prove it.

Jimmy swayed away from it and launched himself forward, grappling with the other man, smothering the movement of his arms then once again thrusting him backwards to keep him off-balance. This day, Jack Temple's superior body weight was overpowered by the aggression that had been intensifying within Jimmy Carson since he'd heard of the death of his friend.

With a thud, Jack Temple's back crashed against the solid timbers again and he sank to his knees as the wind was driven out of him. On the ground he found a large rock, picked it up and came again at Jimmy. If the blow he threw with his rock-filled right hand had connected, it would have broken the younger man's jaw, but Jimmy was able to evade the other man's clumsiness and stepped inside the swinging arm. Although the punch missed his head, he felt the weight of the blow on his back. Still, it didn't prevent him from sinking his own fist into the pit of his opponent's stomach.

Jack Temple grunted and would have fallen to the ground, but Jimmy Carson held him upright, able to smash a blow into his face. It ripped a long slash into the soft skin below Jack's left eye and sent a slick of blood arcing high into the air.

Another grunt escaped from Jack Temple's mouth, but Jimmy Carson was mistaken if he thought the head punch had put an end to the fight. Jack had held on to the rock and as he slumped against the timbers of the corral he amassed all his strength and swung it at the younger man's body. The blow landed just below the heart. Jimmy was momentarily crippled, not only by the intense pain but also by the expulsion of breath from his body. He toppled forward onto the other's shoulders and they both sprawled on the ground.

Their joint suffering presented a brief respite in the fight. Jack Temple was first to recognize the opportunity to finish off his opponent. He shrugged his shoulders and worked his way out from underneath. Gaining his feet, he aimed a kick towards the same spot below the heart where the rock had done its damage. Using his left arm, Jimmy blocked the other's attack then launched his own by grabbing and twisting Jack Temple's foot. As he fell, Jack's head struck one of the cross-timbers, gashing his brow, creating a flow of blood above his eye that mingled with that from the wound below.

Jimmy knelt astride the other's chest.

Gripping the front of Jack's grimy shirt, he used it to haul his head off the ground. 'Stay away from Mrs Danvers,' he shouted, emphasising his warning with another blow to the jaw.

Beth Danvers rested a restraining hand on the younger man's shoulder. 'It's over,' she told him. 'I don't think he has any fight left in him.'

It was true. Jack Temple was stretched out on the ground, unconscious. Jimmy stood and looked at Beth Danvers. It occurred to him that he had no idea what had caused the bruising fight but there was no opportunity for enlightenment. From the direction of the main street a voice arose. Clarion clear, the shout was both a warning and a call to arms.

'They're coming.'

12

Benny Gates was not acting as a lookout when he leant against the tree at the edge of town. He'd merely paused there to smoke a hand-rolled cigarette, hoping that the lonely walk and rough tobacco would amend his mood. Such was the atmosphere in the middle of town, such the threat of violence and reckoning hanging over the place, that even the noise from the drinking places seemed unnaturally muted. Throughout Stanton, citizens had forsaken their normal routines and restless men were seeking quiet places to await the eruption of the looming event in whatever form it took. No one, however, not even Mort Risby and his crew, anticipated that it would involve a force from the Diamond-H descending upon the town. There was no reason to suppose that news of Tom Hoag's current predicament had reached his father. Yet, when Benny's attention was caught by the rising dust that showed across the low grasslands south of town, he had no hesitation in identifying its source. Distance and the oncoming night meant that the riders were nothing more than black silhouettes, menacing shadows, but apart from the Triple-R, only the Diamond-H had the ability to amass so large a crew. Instantly, that weight of unknown expectancy was shed from his shoulders. They were coming, riding fast and with purpose; they were coming for a fight.

Benny Gates ran down the street towards the marshal's office, shouting out the news that a bunch of riders was approaching the town. Those citizens who heard Benny's words as a warning, began to clear the street, taking refuge in the River Bend or another drinking venue along the street. Glasses were filled, lamps were dimmed, and men and women jostled for positions that offered the best views of the street. Anxious though they were to avoid flying lead, they were yet curious enough to hang around to witness the anticipated bloody battle.

Of course, it wasn't Benny's main intention to act as a herald for the residents of Stanton nor to carry the news to Silas Tasker. Primarily, he was yelling a war cry, a call to arms for his boss and the other Triple-R riders. He had left them at the far end of the street, gathered on the boardwalk opposite the marshal's office where Tom Hoag remained. Their nerves, stretched by the chase that had brought them back to town, had been tightened by the hours of inactivity forced on them by the protection Marshal Tasker was currently providing for their quarry. Extra men had been brought in from the ranch and an expectation had grown within the group that when darkness fell, Mort Risby would order the storming of the law office. Tom Hoag would suffer the same fate as that which had befallen young Walt. Now, however, the sight of Benny Gates running down the street, spurred the belief that a different fight was closer at hand.

They surrounded their comrade as he spilled his news to their boss. Instantly, everyone checked their arms and began to make their way towards the other end of the street, seeking places that offered cover for the coming confrontation.

But Mort Risby ordered one man to remain in the shadows opposite the marshal's office. Chuck Grainger was the chosen man because he was proclaimed the best shot in the outfit.

'Silas Tasker will come running when the shooting begins,' Mort told his top hand. 'Perhaps Tom Hoag, too. If you get a clear shot at him, shoot to kill.'

Inside the marshal's office, Abe Brewster had joined Tom Hoag and Silas Tasker. Tom's reason for riding to Stanton after working with the fence crew had been to consult the doctor about his father's rancorous behaviour.

'He's always held Mort Risby responsible for the flare-up that brought you to town,' Tom told Silas.

'He agreed to a ceasefire for the sake of the community, but he never forgot that he lost stock and very nearly lost that stretch of land at Musselshell Valley. He'd mention it from time to time, but it hasn't been an issue since the Triple-R began using a different route. Their cattle are never herded in that direction, but I guess the roots of his mistrust and dislike of the Risbys are deeper than I knew. No doubt Ma and then Mary were responsible for keeping his rancour in check, but Mary's death seems to have knocked all reason out of him. He just won't listen to anyone.'

'He listened to your brother. Frank's identification of Walt Risby kicked off this whole business.'

Tom shook his head. 'He didn't listen to Frank, he latched on to something my brother said, then built it into something he wanted to believe. All Frank said was that he'd followed a horse with a white tail and ever since he's been trying to persuade Pa that it wasn't Walt.'

Tom looked at Abe Brewster, asked the question that had been burning in his brain all day. 'Has Pa gone crazy?

He's like a dog that's been lying in the midday sun. Just wants to snarl and bite at anyone who comes near.'

'Grief, Tom,' the medic replied. 'There's no guarantee what effect it will have on anyone because no one knows what thoughts lurk in another man's head. Your pa spurned help when he was younger, making him a loner and he became more reclusive when your ma died. I don't know any treatment for what ails him.' He paused, thinking. 'Perhaps it is a form of insanity, perhaps only temporary, but I can't cure it.'

'Insanity or not,' Silas Tasker announced, 'I reckon he'll have to stand trial for the hanging of Walt Risby. He's thrown this town into uproar and he's got to answer for it.'

At that moment, the attention of the men in the room was gripped by the sound of raised voices penetrating from beyond the office walls. The street door opened and a townsman peered inside.

'Better come, marshal. Ben Hoag's coming to town with a small army and the Triple-R boys are heading down the street to confront them. There's going to be bloodshed.'

The three men in the room moved rapidly; Silas Tasker had a town to defend, Tom Hoag had family and workers to consider and Doc Brewster was aware that his skills might be in high demand before this day was ended.

Once again, Silas reached for a shotgun as he passed the gun rack that was affixed to the wall near the door. He broke it, checked that it was loaded then snapped it closed again. Before he got outside, however, he was stopped by the arrival of another man at his door.

'This just came through,' Jethro Humbo said, thrusting a short telegraph message into the marshal's hand.

Silas took it but with his mind fully engaged by the possibility of gunplay on his town's main street, he made to push the paper into his shirt pocket while he dealt with the more pressing problem.

'Better read it, Silas,' the man from the post office told him. 'It's the reply you've been waiting for from Sheriff Brown in Miles City.'

Silas took a moment to read the message before pushing it unceremoniously into a pocket. He stepped onto the boardwalk and began following Jethro Humbo who was half-a-dozen steps ahead, hurrying back to his place of business. The drumming sound that reached the marshal's ears announced the arrival of the Diamond-H riders at the edge of town. He quickened his pace, eager to get to the centre of the action before bullets were fired. He spotted Mort Risby's men at various points along the street, some crouching in doorways, others lurking at the corner of buildings. All had their weapons pointed in the direction of the incoming riders.

A shot rang out, the tell-tale flash showing Silas the doorway where the shooter crouched.

He yelled, 'Hold your fire,' but the words were lost in the activity at the far end of the street where horses were objecting to the abrupt halt demanded by their riders and, amid shouts of 'Ambush' and 'Take cover', those same men were scrambling out of their saddles in order to become smaller targets. Another shot was fired. Surprisingly, this one was much closer to Silas, coming from across the street. The marshal heard a grunt and saw Tom Hoag slump back against the office wall. Instantly, Silas grasped the situation, realized that a Triple-R man had remained in the darkness of the opposite veranda in anticipation of a clear shot at Tom. Mort Risby had calculated that the arrival of Ben Hoag would draw them from the office and had posted a sharpshooter to exact full revenge for the death of his son.

The unmistakeable click of a gun being cocked reached him. The gunman was lining up another shot at his target to be certain that his victim was dead. Without hesitation, Silas twisted his body so that his shotgun pointed into the opposite shadows. There was no time to raise it to his shoulder, he pulled the trigger while it was still waist-high. The kick was powerful, the roar loud and the scattering of its load deadly. The gunman was flung back, his broken and lifeless body scattering those seats and tables that had recently been used by the riders of the Triple-R. Then there was silence.

Silas was unable to resist an urge to look back towards his office. Abe Brewster was bent over Tom Hoag but the marshal didn't know if the young cattleman was alive or dead. His duty, however, was to protect the town; it was imperative that he put a stop to the impending battle and was forced to leave the treatment of Tom Hoag in the doctor's hands.

As was common, the shotgun report had a calming effect on those men who could expect little personal gain from the struggle at hand. Many of those who had been in offensive positions were now watching the approaching marshal, their guns held with less enthusiasm than they had been moments earlier. To maintain their attention and to ensure that Ben Hoag and his men were aware of his arrival at the scene, he discharged the other barrel in the air, allowing its sound to dominate the street.

'I want every man to put his gun down,' he shouted, occupying the centre of the street at a point somewhere between the two forces. Onlookers thought their marshal had lost his senses. He presented an open target to both sets of fighters. Silas, however, figured he was in danger of being shot only by the two protagonists. Only Ben Hoag and Mort Risby had enough reason to continue this fight. Subduing them would put an end to the whole business, but subduing them wasn't his aim. He had reason to arrest both men, which was his intention.

Silas first spoke to the people from the Triple-R. 'Put your guns away,' he told them. 'There'll be no more gunplay in this town. I'll arrest any man who doesn't immediately re-holster his six-shooter or put down his long gun.'

Mort Risby strutted forward, pistol in hand. 'This is none of your business, Tasker,' he said. 'Ben Hoag killed my son and he has to pay for that.'

'It's Marshal Tasker to you, Mr Risby,' Silas told him, evoking the rancher's earlier haughtiness, 'and anything that happens in this town is my business. So, unless you want me to crack your head open with this shotgun, I suggest you put your pistol away.'

Mort Risby stared at Silas Tasker. It was the second time in a few hours that he'd spoken to him like a rowdy child in front of his men. For a long moment he stood toe to toe with the lawman, knowing those that rode for him would be swayed by what he did next. He knew the shotgun was an empty threat, both shells had been fired, but, if he shot the marshal, he would be open to a volley from the Diamond-H force. Ben Hoag would be able to justify killing him as the slayer of the town's peacekeeper. He slipped his gun into its holster.

'What about those men?' he asked, pointing to where Ben Hoag and his crew had taken refuge. 'They are armed, too.'

'Mr Hoag,' Silas called, 'tell your men

to put away their guns then come here.'

Townspeople, amazed by the bravery or foolhardiness of their marshal, began to leave their places of refuge. They watched from the sidewalks as Ben approached with Frank a couple of steps behind.

'Where's my son?' asked Ben.

'He's back there.' Silas indicated his distant office with his head. 'Doc Brewster is with him.'

The last words startled Ben Hoag. 'Is my boy hurt?'

'I'm not sure.'

Ben Hoag glared at Mort Risby. 'You'll pay if anything's happened to my boy,' he declared.

'He'll answer to the law,' Silas told him. 'If Tom's dead,' he said to Mort Risby, 'you'll be charged with murder.'

Mort Risby tilted his head higher, as though dismissing the threat as a charge that would never be pursued. 'And what about my boy?' he asked. 'Are you going to charge Ben Hoag with his murder?'

'He killed my daughter,' Ben snapped

back before Silas could respond. 'He deserved to die.'

'No, he didn't, Mr Hoag,' Silas told him, 'and although I haven't the authority to charge you with a crime that took place outside the town limits, I will be advising the state authorities of the lynching of Walt Risby. You will be charged with murder.'

'He killed my daughter,' insisted Ben Hoag.

'Walt Risby had nothing to do with the blaze that destroyed your barn.' Silas withdrew from his pocket the telegraph message that Jethro Humbo had delivered. 'This is irrefutable proof that Walt Risby was in Miles City that night.'

If Silas expected Ben Hoag to accept Sheriff Brown's information without argument, he was mistaken.

'Went to Miles City but didn't stay there. My boy here saw him and followed him all the way to the Dearborn.'

A figure staggered forward, his face battered and bloody, his clothes dishevelled, torn and stained from a bruising struggle.

'Frank Hoag didn't follow anyone to the Dearborn that night,' Jack Temple said. When he had everyone's attention, he imparted the information that was his revenge for the beating he'd taken. 'He was here, in Stanton. Keeping company with that man's wife while he was out of town.' His outstretched arm pointed at Joe Danvers who had left his account books to witness the end of the confrontation outside his store.

There was a moment of silence before Ben turned to his youngest son from whom he expected to hear a vehement denial. No such words were issued and all those who were now looking at Frank, knew that they never would be. Even in the dim evening light Frank Hoag's pallor was obvious to all. His eyes had widened, his stare conveying his nervousness and shame.

The next few seconds were a blur of action. Simultaneously, each of the major participants understood the significance of the new information. Mort

Risby's belief in his son's innocence was vindicated but that only heightened the injustice of Walt's cruel death. The fury that had been building within him since his boy's body had been brought to Stanton, was ready to erupt.

For the first time since Mary's death, the thoughts in Ben Hoag's head were clear and he knew himself guilty of hanging an innocent man.

He'd allowed false information to stoke the fire of bitter loss into hatred. He'd been deceived by his own son. Darkening features told their own tale. He could not let his son's transgression go unpunished.

Silas Tasker witnessed the transformation in each man. So intense were the emotions wrought by the shift in their understanding that they couldn't keep their need for vengeance from their face. For a moment, he'd thought he'd had control of the situation, that there would be no more violence this night. He had been so close to sending the opposing forces back to their respective ranches without further shooting. In the cold light of the following day, when he was more certain of Tom Hoag's condition, he would have ridden out to the Triple-R to arrest Mort Risby, but in a moment that all became an impossibility.

A tic in Mort Risby's left eye and a twist of Ben Hoag's lip sent the message that this night would not end without more bloodshed. It was clear that whatever grievances had been harboured and allowed to fester over the years would be forever resolved for these two men here on this dirty street.

'I'll shoot the first man who touches his gun,' Silas shouted, a vain attempt to defuse the situation. He dropped the shotgun and reached for the Colt at his side.

It was doubtful if either rancher heard him because their hands were already filled with iron. Guns roared, not only those of the three men in the middle of the street but one or two riders from both ranches fired shots across the street. Whose bullet killed which man was unclear but three men lay dead in the street, Ben and Frank Hoag and Mort Risby. A fourth man, Jack Temple, had a nick in his arm which added greatly to the amount of blood he lost that day.

It was Abe Brewster, discharging both barrels of a shotgun he'd borrowed from the marshal's office, who brought about the ceasefire. Silas Tasker, unsure how he'd escaped any injury, ordered the cowboys back to their respective ranches. He'd scrutinised every face, would name them all in the report he would prepare for the town register and would call them all for trial if criminal proceedings became necessary. He thought it unlikely. There didn't seem to be anything to gain when the heads of both outfits were dead.

Despite the banishment of the cow-boys, the drinking palaces were busy that night, the townsmen chewing over every detail of the day's events. It was a profitable night for Noah Pink, too, but he didn't gloat, his face maintained the glum expression that was well-known in Stanton. He had five bodies to attend to in his parlour; two father and son combinations were a unique occurrence. The fifth man was Chuck Grainger who had been struck in the chest by the blast from Silas Tasker's shotgun.

Jack Temple had been patched up and dismissed with a scowl of disapproval by Abe Brewster. Perhaps the barber wasn't altogether to blame for the gunfight that had occurred in the little town, but he'd blackened a woman's name in a most public manner and that didn't sit easy with the medic. Silas Tasker didn't ask Jack Temple to expound on his accusation that Frank had been with Beth Danvers when he was supposed to be chasing a fire-raiser south to the river, but the woman herself arrived at the marshal's office to give him the details.

Abe Brewster was there when Beth arrived; he'd arranged to take Tom Hoag back to the Diamond-H in his buggy. Chuck Grainger's bullet had smashed into the young rancher's left shoulder. He was in pain, but Abe prophesised a full recovery. Beth Danvers had no objection to Abe and Tom remaining while she told her story.

'The first thing you should know,' she began, 'is that Joe isn't my husband. He's my brother. For some reason Gus Hubber told everyone we were husband and wife, before we arrived to replace him. I don't know what his purpose was but I've since heard him referred to as cantankerous so presumably he was hoping to cause some mild mischief. Nonetheless, Joe and I should have corrected the mistake but I must confess we were amused by the conversation of several of the customers who believed we were married. It was wrong of us,' she said, 'and from tomorrow we'll repair the misconception.'

When Silas muttered, 'I won't be pressing criminal charges,' it surprised Abe Brewster, not because he'd expected the lawman to throw the young woman in one of his cells but because he seldom showed a humorous side to his character. The medic attributed it to the aftermath of the violence that Silas had survived.

Beth Danvers responded with a wry smile and seemed a bit more relaxed when she continued her story. 'The other thing you should know,' she looked directly at Tom Hoag, 'is that your brother was very unhappy. We'd talked a couple of times and he'd confided that he'd spent enough time working cattle. It seems wrong to criticise your father tonight, but Frank believed he was considered worthless. He came that night to say goodbye. He'd had another argument with your father and had decided to leave the ranch. He'd heard tales about San Francisco and that was his destination.'

Tom Hoag was unable to refute the woman's words.

'Where does Jack Temple come into this?' Silas wanted to know.

'It was wrong of me, I suppose, to invite Frank in for coffee when Joe was away,' Beth said, 'especially late at night, but he needed to share his secret. I couldn't turn him away. Jack Temple must have seen him arrive and made an assumption that there was something more involved than chatter. He's been trying to pressure me into an association with him ever since. Tonight, he tried to force himself on me, but Jimmy Carson prevented it. I guess his outburst was meant to paint me as a scarlet woman and have me driven out of town.'

'No need for that to happen,' said Silas, 'no need at all.'

Three days later, Silas left his office to lean against a veranda post. He'd begun to get into the habit of doing that at this early hour. In a while, he would cross the street and enjoy breakfast at Minnie's Eatery then take a tray back to feed his prisoners. It was going to be a warm day. He looked down the street, one or two men were making an early start, heading out of town to work at the timber-yard or one of the small farms. The saddle-maker was opening his door and Bart Martin, the River Bend barman, was swilling a bucket of dirty water onto the street after washing the dust from the barroom floor. Normality was returning to Stanton.

Cora Hope was making her way down from the church, head up, eyes searching for a neighbour, any neighbour upon whom she could impose her unholy views. Silas figured she'd have plenty of words to spread this day because yesterday had been a busy one for her husband: he'd spoken over the graves of three men.

He hadn't buried the Hoags, of course. Tom had had his father and brother buried next to his mother and sister. He hadn't been able to dig their graves himself, but he'd stood while his men bent their backs. Ben and Frank were still in Noah Pink's boxes when they were put in the ground. Silas hadn't gone out to the ranch, he wasn't sure he would have been welcome, but Abe and Alice Brewster had attended.

Silas could see Abe Brewster's buggy coming into town past the church. He waited until the doctor drew alongside the veranda and halted.

'Where have you been so early in the morning?'

'The Richardson's farm. Delivered Martha of a girl. Both well.'

Silas nodded. It seemed like a good start to the day.

'People come and people go,' Abe said. 'Which reminds me, I saw Jack Temple leave town yesterday. Do we need a new barber?'

'Reckon so. The judge will be in town next week to try Luke Bywater and Steve Tumbrell. I told Jack Temple I would put him up before the judge for assaulting Beth Danvers if he didn't get out of town.' Silas was pleased that Jack Temple had chosen to leave. He was sure that Cora Hope's subsequent gossip would have twisted every detail that was revealed in court to demean Beth. 'How is Tom Hoag managing with his arm in a sling?' he asked as the doctor prepared to drive on.

'Fine, just fine. I reckon I won't need to visit him more than once a week now.'

'The wound must be healing fast.'

'No faster than any other, but he's got a nurse to keep an eye on it.'

'Really!'

'Clara Buxton. My Alice reckons there'll be wedding bells soon. Nice girl, Clara.'

At that moment, Silas's attention strayed from Abe Brewster. He looked down the street and raised his hat slightly in salute. Beth Danvers was sweeping the entrance porch of the general store. She paused, smiled then returned to the chore.

'Another nice girl,' said Abe Brewster who had witnessed the brief exchange. 'A good woman. Yessir, a good woman.'

We do hope that you have enjoyed reading this large print book.

Did you know that all of our titles are available for purchase?

We publish a wide range of high quality large print books including:
Romances, Mysteries, Classics
General Fiction
Non Fiction and Westerns

Special interest titles available in large print are:
The Little Oxford Dictionary
Music Book, Song Book
Hymn Book, Service Book

Also available from us courtesy of Oxford University Press:
Young Readers' Dictionary
(large print edition)
Young Readers' Thesaurus
(large print edition)

For further information or a free brochure, please contact us at:
Ulverscroft Large Print Books Ltd.,
The Green, Bradgate Road, Anstey,
Leicester, LE7 7FU, England.
Tel: (00 44) 0116 236 4325
Fax: (00 44) 0116 234 0205

Other titles in the
Linford Western Library:

GUNFIGHT AT THE NAMELESS VILLAGE

Chris Adam Smith

Harry James Luck--Civil War veteran, US Cavalry captain; gambler, sometime lawman, and part-time drunk--resigns his commision and heads south to the High Plains country of Texas. There, he meets the lovely Bonnie Luxford, buys a ranch, and hopes to settle down to a peaceful life. But Texas trails never run straight, and a wandering band of Comancheros brings his dream to a fire-ravaged close. Now Harry sets his sights on a new road--a trail of revenge...